Rotten to the Core 2

**Lock Down Publications and Ca$h
Presents**

Rotten to the Core 2
A Novel by *Ghost*

Lock Down Publications
P.O. Box 870494
Mesquite, Tx 75187

Copyright 2018 by Ghost Rotten to the Core 2
www.lockdownpublications.com

First Edition October 2018
Printed in the United States of America

*This is a work of fiction. Names, characters, places, and
incidents either are products of the author's imagination or
are used fictitiously. Any similarity to actual events or
locales or persons, living or dead, is entirely coincidental.*

Lock Down Publications
Like our page on Facebook: Lock Down Publications @
www.facebook.com/lockdownpublications.ldp
Cover design and layout by: **Dynasty Cover Me**
Book interior design by: **Shawn Walker**

Stay Connected with Us!

Text **LOCKDOWN** to 22828 to stay up-to-date with new releases, sneak peaks, contests and more…

Thank you!

Submission Guideline.

Submit the first three chapters of your completed manuscript to ldpsubmissions@gmail.com, subject line: Your book's title. The manuscript must be in a .doc file and sent as an attachment. Document should be in Times New Roman, double spaced and in size 12 font. Also, provide your synopsis and full contact information. If sending multiple submissions, they must each be in a separate email.

Have a story but no way to send it electronically? You can still submit to LDP/Ca$h Presents. Send in the first three chapters, written or typed, of your completed manuscript to:

LDP: Submissions Dept
Po Box 870494
Mesquite, Tx 75187

DO NOT send original manuscript. Must be a duplicate.

Provide your synopsis and a cover letter containing your full contact information.

Thanks for considering LDP and Ca$h Presents.

Ghost

Chapter 1
Jayden

Whitney bounced back into my lap, giving my penis more access into her womb. Her wet walls sucked at me while I held her hips and straightened my back, plunging into her pussy with my eyes closed. She moaned up under me and encouraged me to fuck her harder. "Un, un, yes, daddy, fuck me, fuck me, harder, harder, please. It's my birthday, it's my birthday, uhhh, shit, it's my birthday," she hollered, lowering her head to the couch that I had her bent over inside of her mother's living room. She spread her legs wider and continued to drive back into me, matching me pound for pound. Her juices leaked out of her center and ran down her inner thighs, all the way to her ankles.

The constant slapping of our skins resonated loudly. Her ass jiggled every time I crashed into her, trying to become one with her small yet oh so thick frame.

"It's. Yo. Day. Baby. It's. Yo. Day, baby. Uhhh, it's yours lil' mama." I groaned, speeding up the pace, digging my fingers into her small waist to pull her back into me.

She moaned with her mouth wide open. I felt my dick going in and out of her. Her scent wafted up my nostrils, driving me crazy. I had a thing for her, even though she was my right-hand man's little sister. Since Nico had been locked away, me and Whitney had developed a strong relationship. So much so that I felt like I even loved her, and it would be nothing for me to hold her down.

I slammed forward, implanting myself as deep as I could, feeling my climax building. Then, I pulled all the way back just to slam forward again. Afterward, I was going full speed, trying to tear that pussy up. It felt so good, I could no longer control my urge to come deep within her womb. I had to release myself within her body; had to leave her with a piece of me. So, I got to fucking her so hard that I was hurting my stomach, smacking her on that big ass booty while she crashed back into me.

"Daddy, daddy, unnn-a, unn-a, uh, uh, it's, my, birthday! I'm cumming, daddy, I'm cumming, uhhh-a!" She screamed, and implanted herself onto my pipe, slamming backward and keeping her pussy in place, while my penis throbbed deep within her stomach.

I was on the verge of cumming when suddenly I felt something hard slam the back of my head. I froze in place and tried to turn around to see what it was, and that's when I was flung off Whitney and thrown to the floor with my pants down. Before I could get up, Nico rushed to stand over me, aiming a Mossberg pump at my face, with his eyes lowered and a mug on his face.

I looked up and into the barrel of the Mossberg, and all I could do was swallow my saliva and look up into his eyes.

"You bitch ass nigga. You got the nerve to be fucking my baby sister in my mother's house after I told you to stay away from her!" He lowered his eyes and placed his finger on the trigger. "Ain't nothing finna stop me from killing you, nigga. Word is bond." He looked over his shoulder to his sister

Whitney, then his mother Janet who was just coming into the living room to witness what was going on. "Y'all, get the fuck out of here and go upstairs right now. Hurry up!" he ordered, then turned his eyes back down to me. "I'm finna kill this nigga tonight."

I thought about jumping up and attacking him, fighting for my life before he could take me out, because I knew that he was more than capable. Nico was a hot head. A loose cannon. He didn't take to anyone crossing him in any fashion. It didn't matter that we had been best friends ever since we were six years old and had been inseparable ever since then. Or the fact that ever since he'd been locked up, I'd paid all his mother's bills and made sure she came and visited him four times a week. I'd also dropped fifty gees to get him a lawyer and made sure that while he was on the inside that his books were more than straight. No, none of that mattered. The only thing that mattered was that I had crossed him by fucking with his sister, and not posting his bail when he'd ordered me to. I knew that I was in a life or death situation, and I didn't see any way out of it, so I had to respond as best as I knew how.

"Y'all, go! I'm not gon' say it again!" He hollered, looking down on me, taking the barrel of the Mossberg and leveling it so that it was aimed right between my eyes.

Before I could make a move to get out of the impossible situation, Whitney ran over and pushed the barrel of his gun away from me, then laid on me with her back on my chest. "No, Nico, you can't kill him. I'm pregnant with his baby. You can't do this." She cried, turning over and hugging me, laying her head on my chest, and looking at him from the corners of her eyes.

At first, Nico's eyes were low, but at hearing Whitney say that, his eyes grew as big as paper plates, causing the skin on his forehead to move backwards. "You gotta be fucking kidding me, Whitney. You let this bitch ass nigga get you pregnant?" He yelled through clenched teeth. Then, he grabbed her arm, trying to yank her from my body, but she held on to me for dear life. "Get the fuck off of him. I'm finna blow this nigga's head off, and you getting rid of that baby. You ain't bringing no turn-coat into this world. I can't believe yo' stupid ass." He yanked her with all of his might, pulling her away from me.

"Nooo!" She screamed, digging her nails into my shoulder blades, then dragging them across my neck, cutting me open.

My blood ran out of me almost immediately. The cuts stung like crazy.

Soon as Whitney was to her feet, she slapped Nico across the face so hard that spit flew out of his mouth, and off instinct he returned her slap with a brutal one of his own. It was so hard that she did a 180 and fell onto the glass table in his mother's living room, shattering it, and causing glass to fly everywhere.

Janet ran into the room toward the fallen Whitney. "Oh my God, Nico, what have you done?" She screamed.

"Mama, she hit me first, then I—"

I bounced from the carpet and rushed Nico, picking him up by the waist and running full speed with him right into the wall where we crashed, and he dropped the Mossberg.

Boom! Fire spat from its barrel. The bullet slammed into the front window, blowing it out. The curtains that covered it had a big hole in the middle of them, and they waved back and forth as the wind from outside attacked them.

I had Nico in a bear hug. He cocked his head back and then brought it forward, slamming it into my nose and mouth, busting both of them wide open. I tasted my own blood right away, before releasing him and falling backward.

"You bitch ass nigga." He grabbed my shirt and swung a right hook, crashing his fist into my jaw, knocking me over the couch.

I fell right beside Janet and Whitney, trying to regain my composure. My face was stinging along with my ribs. I felt like I couldn't breathe, and I kept on swallowing heavy portions of my own blood, so much so that I was starting to choke until I hawked a big loogey and spat it out on to the carpet. Then, Nico was grabbing me again by the back of my shirt.

"Y'all, stop it! Stop this shit, Nico; you're killing him!" Janet said, trying to help her daughter to sit up.

Nico pulled me up and attempted to lift me over his head. I snapped out of it. As he bent down to lift me, I brought my knee up to his face, then pushed him backward, and hit him with a two piece— one to the jaw and the second blow caught him under the chin. I wrapped my arms around him, lifted him into the air and dumped him on his back with a loud boom, then let him go. He writhed on the carpet in pain.

His face scrunched into a mug. "You bitch ass nigga, now I'm really finna kill you," he said out of breath. Blood leaked out of the corner of his mouth. His jaw began to swell upon his yellow face.

I took a step back and my foot landed on the Mossberg pump. I leaned down to pick it up when he kicked me dead in the face. I saw blue lightning as I grabbed the Mossberg and flew backward with it in my hands. Even though I felt dizzy, I was ready to blow this nigga's head off, right hand man or not. He tried to pull the Mossberg away from me, and I slid my finger to the trigger and started to squeeze it again and again, ready to see his body fill up with holes, but nothing happened.

I cocked it and pulled the trigger, over and over, still no popping occurred. I was confused.

Nico straddled me and punched me in the face. "You fucked my sister, nigga. Left me to rot in prison. I told you what it was." He swung again.

Blocking him, I grabbed the back of his head and pulled it forward, head-butting him like he'd done me. I heard his nose crunch before he fell backward. Then there was the sound of sirens blaring down the block before a police car came and slammed on its brakes right in front of Janet's house. A second later, there was another, then two seconds after that one, another one.

I pushed Nico off me and stood up, buckling my belt and running to the back of the house, where I opened the door and nearly fell down the stair to the last door. I opened it, running out into the night with blood running out of my nose and mouth. I couldn't breathe, nor could I think straight. I didn't know where I was going or what I was going to do. I just started running at full speed while the wind blew into my face, further taking my breath away. I looked over my shoulder right as I got into the alley behind Janet's house, and saw Nico run out of her back door in my direction. He constantly looked over his shoulder in a state of panic. Within seconds he was a few paces behind me.

I thought he still wanted to fight, so I stopped and held up my guards. "What's hannin', nigga? We ain't finna keep playing these games." I stepped forward and swung at him wildly. I was so dizzy from the blood running out of my nose that I could barely balance myself on my feet. All it would have took was for him to connect with one punch and I would have been laid out in that alley.

He blocked my assault, then pushed me as hard as he could, sending me staggering into a big metal garbage can. "Gone, bitch ass nigga. I ain't got time for that right now!" He hollered, looking over his shoulder again. "I ain't going back to prison for nobody. I'll deal with you later. You best believe I'm bodying yo' ass in due time. That's on my mother." He nodded. "Yeah, you gon' get yours." Blood ran out of his nose into his mouth. He dabbed at it with his fingers, coating them with the liquid.

I got my footing, saw a two by four with a big nail sticking out of it, and picked it up. "N'all, fuck that. We gon' do this now!" I said, rushing toward him with the board. I swung it, just as he turned around. The block of wood slammed into his back along with the nail and got stuck.

"Arrghhhh!" He hollered, turning in a circle, trying to get the nail and board out of him.

I thought about rushing him right then, fucking him up, and stomping his head into the concrete of the alley, killing him and getting it over with.

"Hey! Freeze! Philadelphia Police!" A uniformed officer hollered, coming out of Janet's yard with his gun drawn and pointed directly at me. "Don't move!"

I raised my hand in the air, ready to surrender, then he fired a round. His bullet smashed into the big metal garbage can right beside me, just as his partner came alongside him, kneeled and got ready to shoot. I ducked behind the garbage can, then hit it up the gangway that it was behind. I found myself in one of the neighbors' backyards, running for my life with the police running behind me. My heart pounded in my chest, my lungs felt like they were filled with ice water, and on top of that my nose wouldn't stop bleeding. It dripped from my chin and onto the pavement. I looked over my shoulder as another round was fired. The bullet whizzed past my ear in a loud pee-yoon sound.

"Freeze, motherfucker! Stop running!" One of the officers ordered behind me.

I could hear their feet stomping the grounds behind me. Though I'd only seen two of them, it sounded like there were way more than that. One of them got on his radio and told the dispatcher our location.

I ran from the backyard, out to the front of the neighbor's house and kept on running. The block where Janet lived was flooded with police cruisers.

I'd made a big mistake by running back on to it, because as soon as I got there, I felt trapped, but I didn't stop running. I ran across that street and back alongside of another gangway that led to an alley. Once there, I broke down it with the police right behind me, yelling for me to stop. I ignored them and ran as fast as I could toward the busy avenue. I knew that if I had any chances of surviving without them shooting me down in the street, I'd have to get to where there were plenty of witnesses, and that's just what I did.

I ran into the middle of the busy intersection where cars where speeding past on each side; their horns blowing at me to get out of the way. I threw my hands in the air and got down on my knees, right below the traffic lights for all to see.

It didn't take long before I was kicked in the back and forced to my stomach by a police officer. "When we tell you to stop running, you stop, you dumb nigger." He threw his forearm in the back of my neck and rubbed my face into the concrete of the street.

Another ran over and kicked me right between the legs, sending my balls into my stomach. I hollered out in pain before I felt him twisting my wrist, pulling it way up my back. "You son of a bitch. I don't like running. You got my deodorant wearing off of me." He punched me in the back of the head and forced my face into the concrete, taking over for his partner who was putting handcuffs on my wrists so tight that I felt like he was cutting into them with a knife.

"Say, man, you putting them cuffs on too tight. I can't feel my fingers!" I hollered with my face stinging worse than I ever remembered. I laid like that in a puddle of my own blood.

"Shut up, you dumb son of a bitch! Maybe next time you'll listen when you're given a command by an authority figure." He clicked them tighter and smacked me in the back of the head, before pulling me to my feet. "Get your ass up. You're toast."

As soon as I was on my feet, it was like every injury that I had came to the forefront. I was in so much pain that I couldn't walk. I could barely breathe. My knees gave out on me and I fell while the officer was still holding me, down to the concrete.

Instead of him helping me up he snapped. "That's it." He threw me to the ground, took out his billy club and whacked me across the back with it so hard that I fell onto my stomach. "You're going to listen." He whacked me again, this time twice as hard as before.

"Aw, fuck, you punk ass muthafucka!" I hollered, looking around at the traffic jam that we'd caused. People were standing outside of their cars with their phones out, recording the entire scene.

The police's partner joined in, kicking me in the ribs, just as three more police ran over to help them whoop me. "Stop resisting. Stop resisting," they said this again and again, though I was barely able to move a muscle.

"Y'all ain't gotta do him like that!" said a heavy-set sista with her phone recording us. She was parked under the lights with her driver's side door wide open, getting the best possible angle that she could. Beside her were other drivers and witnesses doing the same thing.

But we were in Philly, so the police paid her no mind. They kept right on whooping my ass until I passed out. When I woke up the first time, I was on a stretcher being rushed into the emergency room. I felt like I was choking on my own blood, so I passed back out. When I woke up the second time, I was being worked on by a room full of hospital staff. I passed out again, and the third time I woke up to see one of my wrists handcuffed to the hospital bed. I was so high that I felt no pain. I looked all around the blurry room, seeing the two police officers looking down on me with their mouths moving, but I couldn't make sense of the words coming out of them. My eyes rolled into the back of my head and I passed out again with visions of a pregnant Whitney flashing through my mind.

Ghost

Chapter 2

I found out that I stayed in the hospital for three weeks straight, in a coma and under arrest. When I finally came to, I was whisked off to the county jail and booked in for fleeing and alluding a police officer, and battery to a police officer. I didn't know where the fuck that charge came from when they were the ones that beat me down, and the final reason I was booked into the county jail was for the investigation of two counts of first-degree intentional homicide. At hearing this charge, I damn near lost my mind. I threw up in my mouth and had to swallow it.

The authorities took me right to the hole, which was a small room with no window and no mattress, just a concrete slab and a dirty ass metal toilet and sink that was combined as one unit. The water inside of the toilet was a dark brown, and the sink was so dirty that I refused to go near that muhfucka. It looked like whoever had been in there before me took their shits and pisses in the sink, after they'd clogged up the toilet. On top of that, it smelt so bad that it was hard for me to breathe. They kept me in this room for two whole days and didn't even bring me nothing to eat, or drink, even though I don't think I would have been able to eat anything, had they brought it, because of the stench inside of the small room.

The afternoon of the third day, I was awakened by one of the guards kicking on the door. "Hey! Hey! Get your ass up. There are some homicide detectives here that want to speak to you!" The fat red faced man hollered into the skinny window of the door.

I sat up with my back against the wall, weak and a little disoriented. I got to my feet and staggered around a little bit, with my head pounding, walked to the door and waited for him to open it.

He slammed open a food slot in the middle of it, then clicked the handcuffs that were in his hands. "Put your fucking wrists through the trap. You must be restrained. From what I hear, you're an animal." He laughed.

I slid my hands through the trap and allowed for myself to be handcuffed. Once they were on tight and secure, he hollered for my cell to be opened, and I stepped out into the brightly lit hallway. He grabbed me by the right arm and handled me all aggressive like.

I jerked my arms away from him. "You ain't gotta handle me like I'm yo' bitch a something. Fuck, what's with wrong with you?" I asked, looking to my right at him.

He grabbed my arm again and slammed me into somebody else's cell door, placing his mouth on to my ear. "Now, you listen here, you black bastard. You're in my house now. I don't give a fuck who you are in those streets. You're out of your cotton-picking mind if you think you're going to come here and run anything. You got me? In here, I am the boss, and you do what the fuck I say. Now get your shit together quickly, or I'll make you pay a price like you've never seen before." He yanked me back on course and held my right arm so tight while we walked that I wanted to spit in his face, but I was in no position to do so. I had to just chill so I could get the fuck out of that white man's jail. I already knew how Philly got down against black men, and I wasn't trying to become a statistic.

Five minutes later, I was sitting in front of two homicide detectives. One was a dark skinned, heavy-set, older man with a big bald spot in his afro by the name of Jackson. The other was a heavy-set white man, with curly, black hair. He also had a bald spot in the back of his head as well. I took them to be about the age of forty plus. The white man's name was Peretti.

Jackson took a box of Newport's out of his suit jacket pocket and tried to hand me one, but I shook my head. "Why am I in here?" I asked, looking from one cop to the other.

Jackson laughed. "Ah, so you wanna go right in, huh?" He shrugged. "Okay then, let's get to it. Peretti, show him the pictures." He took a cigarette out of the pack, placed it into his mouth, and lit the tip, blowing the smoke into the air, looking across the metal table at me with a grin on his face.

Peretti went into his briefcase and pulled out a stack of eight by eleven sized pictures, laying them flat on the table before me so I could look down at them. "You recognize these people?" he asked, looking up at me.

I nodded. "Yeah, that's Lincoln, but I ain't ever seen the other dude before." I looked up at him. "What you wanna know about him? He's dead?"

Peretti sucked his teeth and nodded. "The other man is his father, and we know they're dead. We also know that you know who killed them. No, let me give you one better. We know that you had something to do with these murders. The streets talk, Jayden, and they are screaming your name. How about you help yourself?"

I scrunched my face. "Yo, I ain't have shit to do with them niggas being killed, and to be honest with you, I don't give a fuck that they're dead. I ain't have no business dealings with neither one of 'em, so life goes on. And fuck what the streets talking about too. You can't believe everything you hear. Nah' mean?"

Jackson laughed and nodded. "Aw, so you are tough. I guess the streets got that part right. Far as us not believing everything we hear, well, we don't. Especially not that bullshit coming out of your mouth right now." He pointed to the table.

Peretti reached over his shoulder and placed seven more pictures onto the table. These were pictures of the murder scene. Both men had been killed viciously. They were left twisted. "Look at these pictures and tell me that you don't feel anything. Look at them!" he hollered before sitting across from me.

"Does irritated count? 'Cause that's the only thing I feel right now. Fuck y'all got me in here asking me these questions for, man? Like I said, I didn't fuck with Lincoln or his pops, and I didn't have nothing against either one of them either. It's fucked up that they got twisted, but life goes on. When is my bail hearing?" I asked, sitting back in my chair.

Jackson blew smoke across the table and into my face. "If I got anything to do with it, you'll never see the streets of Philly again. I wanna bury you so far under the prison that you'll have the earth's magma heating yo' ass." He leaned forward. "Did your cousin Naz do this?" He asked, smiling.

Peretti sat a mugshot of my cousin on the table and slammed his hand on top of it. "We got good intel that says he did these murders, and that you set it up and were the look out. We also found a size eleven and a half bloody foot print in the carpet beside Lincoln's father's body; a foot print that we're sure would match one of yours."

I shrugged. "Mine and a million other niggas in Philly. And, so what? When is my bail hearing? You son of a bitches done already had me for nearly seventy-two hours, so y'all gotta either let me go, or give me a bail hearing. So, which one is it going to be?" I asked, looking from one man on to the next.

Jackson laughed and looked over to Peretti. "Looks like we got us a real live killer here, Peretti. Coldhearted and without trace of fear in his whole body. Boy, I sho' likes me a nice chase, Jayden. I like when you thugs make me work for it. It makes my dick hard." He growled, lowering his eyes.

Now I was laughing. "Seems like you got a boring ass life. When is my bail hearing? Give me that or let me go. I don't know shit about Lincoln's murder, or his pops. That shit ain't got nothing to do with me."

Peretti curled his upper lip. "I find it ironic that as soon as the dirt is thrown on top of his casket, you're fucking his woman and putting a baby inside of her. Looks to me like motive. Well, that and the missing kilos that he'd bought from an undercover federal agent. You know anything about that?"

Even though my heart was pounding in my chest because I was seeing how deep this shit really went, I had to keep my composure and remain calm. I took a deep breath and exhaled slowly. "Well, if you talking about Whitney, yeah, we fucking, and yeah, that's my woman. But I'd never need to kill no nigga just to take his bitch. Me and her got a long history. Ain't no strings there. She's free to do what she pleases, and vice versa." I ran my tongue across my upper row of teeth. "When is my bail hearing? Matter fact, ain't you muhfucka supposed to read me my rights or something? Y'all just breaking every rule in the book, huh? Then got the nerve to try and get information from me when I don't know what the fuck going on. I need a lawyer; how about that?" I said, sitting forward and holding my breath because Jackson kept on blowing that stanky ass smoke into my face.

Peretti took the pictures and put them back into his briefcase without so much as a word.

Jackson continued to smile, then leaned forward in his seat. "As crazy as this sounds, I like you, Jayden. I can tell that you're going to be a nice lil' challenge that I look forward to embracing every single morning until I break your ass down into fractions. You will not defeat me or Peretti." He laughed and nodded, stubbing his cigarette out on the table. "We're going to see to it that you are released. So, go live your life, have fun, but know that nothing is what it seems, and until you're behind bars for the rest of your life, it never will be." He slammed his hand on the table and stood up, looking me in the eyes the entire time.

They left the freezing cold interview room and slammed the metal door behind them. The sounds echoed before fading away, leaving me with my mind racing like crazy. I knew that they had to have gotten their information from Nico. He'd decided to turn bitch and try and to put Lincoln and his father's murder on me and my cousin, just so he could walk free.

A part of me couldn't really believe it that he'd stoop so low, and turn bitch so quick, but then again, he'd told me time and time again that he would get out of prison by any means, and he didn't care who he screwed over to make it happen. Nico was selfish, and I saw that he was going to be a problem. I wondered if they had him locked up, or if he was free and on the streets. I prayed that he was still behind bars like myself, because had he not been, I feared for the safety of my mother.

Nico had already threatened to kill her when he was in prison. He'd said that first he would kill me, and then her. I only hoped that since I was still alive that he was waiting to finish me off before he moved on to her. I couldn't wait to get up with him. I had visions in my head of blowing his head off and stomping it until my Timberlands filled up with his blood. Philly was not big enough for the both of us. Somebody was going to have to die in a bloody fashion so that a statement could be made to the streets when it came to snitching and betrayal.

I stayed up all that night, in my cell, tossing and turning on the concrete slab. The punk ass guards had turned the air conditioner all the way up, but before I'd came back into the room, they'd taken my blankets and sheets away, forcing me to endure the elements. After a while, I jumped up and got to pacing, blowing air into my hands while smoke came out of my mouth because the room was so cold.

I had to get rid of Nico. I had to annihilate him and kill him in a fashion so cold that his death would go down in the history books of Philly's slums. I knew he was going to come at me hard, so I would have to be ready for him and firing on all cylinders.

* * *

The next morning, I was whisked off to my bail hearing and was released after the judge gave me a $2,000 signature bond for the petty charges that I had accrued nearly a month ago. The Public Defender that stood beside me whispered to me that they would wind up dropping all charges against me, as long as I didn't file a civil suit against the county of Philadelphia for police brutality. I was so anxious to get back into the streets that I was willing to sign some paperwork stating that I would not file a civil suit if they dropped all charges.

He had them drawn up two hours later, and before I stepped foot back into the free streets of Philly, I signed them, and the dirty deal was made. Though I would never forget the faces of the police that had done what they had to me, I would get they ass back one day soon, that was for sure.

I had to shield my eyes from the bright sunlight as the guards opened the big metal door and pushed me out of it, while I held a clear plastic bag that contained my Farrago belt, cell phone, and shoe strings inside of it. I had to close my eyes and open them slowly so I could adjust to the outside.

"Sorry, but you gotta walk away from the property while I'm watching you. Get from back here and walk that way. It leads to the front of the building. I'm told that you have a loved one waiting for you there."

I nodded and made my way around the front of the building. I was dizzy again, and I could tell that I had lost some weight because my clothes seemed way bigger than they had before, and I had to hold my pants up with one hand while I tried to walk as fast as I could without passing out. I needed to get some food in my system before I hunted Nico's ass down and killed him.

As I rounded the corner of the county jail, I saw my mother just getting out of her red Mercedes Benz that I'd bought her for her fortieth birthday.

As soon as she saw me, her eyes grew wide and then she was running toward me with her long, curly hair flowing behind her, blowing in the wind. "Baby, baby, baby. Are you alright?" she asked when she got to me, wrapping her arms around my body and squeezing me so tight that I could barely move.

I nodded. "I'm good, ma. You know you raised a solider; can't nothing break me." I said, sounding tougher than I felt. I wanted to let her know how much pain I was in, but I couldn't stand for her to break down over me.

My mother was a tough woman, but when it came to me, she was extremely overprotective and emotional. I was her only child.

She shook her head and blinked tears. They ran down her small, beautiful face, and I stepped forward and wiped them away before kissing her on the forehead. "We're gonna sue these muthafuckas for everything they got. That video of them beating you down in the streets has been all over the news, and some very important people are speaking out about it. They gon' pay for what they did to my child. Then, they had the nerve to not allow for me to see you ever since you've been in this hell hole. Shit, I thought you were dead." She hugged me again and laid her head on my chest briefly, then took a step back and grabbed my hand, leading me to her red Benz.

I walked her around to the driver's side door and opened it for her, waited until she got in, then went around to the passenger's side. By the time I got there, she already had the door opened. I sat in the seat, pulling the seatbelt over me. "I'm good, mama. You ain't gotta stress out about how they handled me because it could have been a lot worse. They could've killed me or something." I shook my head and tossed my plastic bag in the backseat.

She started the car and pulled away from the curb, shaking her head. "Don't even say that, baby. Please don't never say nothin' like that again. I don't know what I would do if something like that happened to you. Those two bullets you took were enough to send me to an early grave. Lord knows I'm not strong enough to endure something happening to my baby. But they gon' pay. I got a good lawyer already, and as of two days ago, the city was talking about settling your case for two million dollars. They don't even wanna fight it. It was all on television, and people put it on YouTube. I think they just want it to go away." She smiled warmly, but it was too late for that." She reached over and squeezed my hand.

I lowered my head and ran my hand over my face. "Two million dollars? Are you sure?" I asked, feeling sick on the stomach.

She nodded with a huge smile on her face now. "Yes, and that's without going to court, so imagine what we'll get if we move to have the officer's prosecuted, and then bring a civil suit against the city. We might get three times that. I've been contacted by so many lawyers that I had to turn my phone off, then I turned it back on because I didn't want to miss your phone call. I'm backed up on emails and voicemails. We're good to go. I didn't want to make not one move without you by my side. Then, those devils decided to keep you in there for nearly four days without allowing for you to contact me. Did they even offer you the phone?" She asked.

My face was red, and I felt like I was getting ready to throw up all over the dashboard. I unbuckled my seatbelt, reached on to the back seat, grabbed my plastic bag full of items, took out the paper' that I'd previously signed, and handed them to her as she rolled to a halt at a red light.

She frowned and looked over at me. "What's this, son?"

"That's two million dollars wasted; that's what it is. For them to let me go, and to drop all charges, they made me sign this paperwork stating that I wouldn't file any charges against the city of Philadelphia, and I would let the matter go. I wanted to get out of there so bad that I signed it, and it's over with. Dang! I wasn't even thinking clearly." I balled my hands into fists and banged them against my forehead while my mother read the paperwork over with a stumped look on her face.

She reached over and pulled my hand into hers, clasping our fingers. Her lips moved as she read the paperwork, line for line. A car pulled up behind us and started to blow its horn. I looked up and saw that we were sitting in front of a green light, and when she acknowledged that fact, she pulled off and folded the paper, placing it into her lap.

"Don't worry, baby. I'm still going to have a few of those lawyers look it over, because from what I'm seeing, they're saying that you're agreeing to not bring charges against the city. It looks to me like the officers that were involved are on their own." She looked over at me and smiled. "We'll figure it out. Mama got you, you know that."

I looked her over for a long time, then nodded. "I know you do, ma. You always have."

Right there, in that moment, I imagined Nico hurting my mother and it made me angry. She was all that I had, and the fact that Nico had threatened her life let me know that shit was real, and he had to go.

Chapter 3

When I walked into my mother's house that day after I'd gotten out of the county jail, I almost had a heart attack when my cousin Myeesha jumped from the side of the door and yelled surprise. My first instincts were to protect my mother, so I wound up rushing into the house and closing the door behind me, leaving her outside in safety, until my brain registered the fact that it was not Nico jumping out at me, but my older cousin. I put my hand over my heart and felt it beating harder that I ever remembered before.

Myeesha ran to me and wrapped her arms around my neck, while my mother beat on the door. "I missed you so much, cousin. I had to come and see you, especially after everything that happened." She said, stepping on her tippy toes to kiss me on the cheek, then looking into my eyes with her natural green ones.

Myeesha was Italian and Black, about 5'2", slightly bow-legged, and built like a stripper from Atlanta. In fact, that is where she was from. She was jazzy, and she and I had been close ever since we were little kids, and I'd spend summers down in Atlanta with her and her siblings. Her father was my mother's half-brother. Myeesha was the type of female that said whatever was on her heart and she rarely cared about how anybody felt about it. On top of that, she was one of those females that acted as if she could have any man, or anything that she wanted out of life. She had boundary issues, and even though she and I were family, she felt that I belonged to her in a sense and got real jealous whenever there was another female around that I was talking to.

I hugged her back, then opened the door for my mother. "I missed you, too. It's been about five years, ain't it?" I asked, ready to sit down. The whole $2-million thing was causing me to become dizzy. I couldn't believe that I had signed away that amount of money. My public defender had screwed me over, like most did men of my color.

My mother came in with her yellow face red with anger. "Damn, soon as this lil' pretty heffa bring her ass up here, you gotta slam the door in my face, huh?" She looked me up and down before shaking her head.

I broke my embrace with Myeesha, even though she was trying to let me go. I turned to my mother and pulled her into my arms, walking out of the room with her. "N'all, it wasn't that, mama. I thought it was somebody else, and off instinct I had to make sure you were good." I exhaled loudly. "It's some things I gotta talk to you about so you can see where I'm coming from."

She looked up at me with a worried expression. "Is everything okay?" She placed her small hand on my chest.

Before I could answer her question, our doorbell rang. Myeesha went and pulled the curtain back, looking on to the porch. "Uh, Jayden, I'm pretty sure that this is one of your lil' broads on the porch. She look too young to be one of my auntie's friends." She looked over her shoulder at me. "You want me to tell her to keep it moving, 'cause I just got here and you ain't spent no time with me yet. I ain't going." She frowned and flared her nostrils.

I hurried out of the dining room and got into the front room before Myeesha could open the door. Looking out of the window, I saw that it was Whitney. She stood on the porch, facing the door in anticipation, wearing a tight purple Prada dress that clung to her every curve. Her curly hair blew in the wind, and more than once she had to pull a strand of it from her cheek.

"Yo, this ain't no broad, this my woman and the mother of my kid right here." I said, opening the door. "Hey, baby."

She rushed inside of the hallway and hugged me tightly before pulling my head down so she could kiss and suck all over my lips. "Daddy, I missed you so much, and they wouldn't let me come in to see you. The whole time you were in your drug induced coma, I was right there by your side until they forced me to leave it. I'm so sorry that you had to go through all of that. Oh, and Nico's out. He says he's going to kill you and I believe him. What are we going to do?" She asked, looking into my eyes.

I closed the door, looking over her shoulder to see if I could detect anything strange outside, but all seemed normal. After locking the door, I wrapped my arm around her lower back and led her further into the house.

Myeesha strolled in the middle of the floor in her tight Burberry skirt and blouse, tapping her bare foot on my mother's carpet with her arms folded, looking Whitney up and down. "Uh, I hope you ain't gon' be needing him all his time because I just flew in from

Atlanta, and I was expecting to catch up with my cousin. I'm passing up a lot of good money to be here, so if you can, can you make this brief?" She tapped her pink Rolex watch, rolled her eyes, and walked off with her skirt hugging that big ass. I could hear her mumbling to herself.

Whitney pointed at her and looked up at me. "Okay, now that was rude. What's her problem?"

I walked over and sat on the couch, pulling her down onto my lap. "Don't worry about her. My cousin just a little nuts and real possessive of me, especially since we ain't seen each other in a long time. She'll be awright though. When did they let Nico out?" I moved a bunch of curls out of her face and placed them behind her ear. After not seeing her for a few weeks, I was reintroduced to the fact of how gorgeous she really was.

"He got out about twenty minutes ago, and my mother went to pick him up. He's still pretty mad about us, Jayden. He feels like you betrayed him, and he says that once your right-hand man betrays you, you must kill him. That it's the law of the land in Philly, whatever that means." She shook her head. "I'll die without you. You're my everything, Jayden. What are we going to do?" She asked, rubbing my cheek.

I leaned forward and kissed her on the stomach through the Prada material that was covering it. "You don't worry about that. How is our baby doing? You been eating the way you're supposed to?"

She lowered her head and shook it. "I ain't gon' even lie. I haven't been able to do anything that I've supposed to, ever since they stripped you away from me. My mind has been a pure wreck. But now that you're home, maybe I can do a better job, long as you help me. I have missed you so freaking much, Jayden."

I picked my head up and kissed her soft lips, rubbing her stomach again. "I know you have, baby, and I have missed you too. I thought about you every second that I was awake. I don't care what I gotta go through with Nico. In the end, it's going to be me and you. I love you way too much. I'd never let you go. You belong to me. Do you understand that?"

She lowered her head and nodded slowly. "Yes, I do. But, baby, Nico is mad. I think he's really going to try and kill you again. He said that if I wasn't his sister that he would kill me for betraying him. And that whenever our baby is born, that he's going to torture it before he kills it. And the look in his eyes told me that he was serious. I've never seen him so mad before, and of course my mother tried to calm him down, but that didn't work. What are we going to do?"

I exhaled and looked into her eyes. "Do you want the truth?"

She nodded. "Yes, because I can't think straight. I need to know your game plan." She held the side of my face affectionately.

I took her wrist and held it in my hand, leaned forward and kissed her stomach again before looking up into her eyes. "Baby, I'm gon' have to kill Nico before he can get a hold of me or our child. It's just the law of the jungle. When a man threatens your life and the life of your seed, you must annihilate him before he can carry out his threats. Do you understand that?"

She blinked tears. "Yes. But he's my brother, I don't want him to die either. I love him." She whimpered, then covered her face with both hands, sobbing into them.

I shook my head and leaned back, running one hand over my waves that were curling up. I needed to get my hair cut soon and I needed to shave. I took her hands away from her face and looked into her eyes. "Whitney, do you remember me tellin' you that when it came down to it you were going to have to choose between me and Nico?"

She wiped her face and nodded. "Yes."

I took my thumb and wiped away a line of snot that had oozed out of her nose. Grabbing a Kleenex from the table, I wiped my thumb then handed her a couple. "And what did you say?"

Her chest heaved, she inhaled deeply, then blew it back out, causing tears to roll down her cheeks. "I said I'd choose you. That it was a no brainer. But I didn't know that it meant that one of you had to die." She lowered her head and broke into a fit of tears with her shoulder going up and down.

I grabbed her to my chest and rubbed her back. "I hate that you in the middle of this, Whitney, but it's a part of the game. Maybe you should just go home and rethink some things. I gotta get my head together anyway. After I do, I'll reach out to you, and we'll figure out which way we'll go." I stood up and that in turn made her do the same.

She shook her head and grabbed a hold of my shirt. "No, please, Jayden. I'm not trying to be away from you again. I love you. You are the father of my unborn child. I'll stand by you over anybody else. I mean that." She cried, wrapping her arms around my neck, and crying into my chest again.

I rubbed her back and held her close. I knew that I was placing her in an impossible situation, but I felt that she should have thought things through more thoroughly before she decided to cross those lines with me. There was no doubt about it. I loved Whitney and I knew for a fact that I would hold her down, and make sure she never needed for anything. I didn't know we'd be on some one on one type shit, or a relationship but I did know that whenever I found myself fully ready that she would be the woman I chose, no matter what took place with Nico. On top of that, I knew that I had to kill her brother. It was no way around it. Nico was a savage, and if I treated him as any less than such, I would be a dead man in no time.

So, I didn't care that the police were supposedly watching me closely, or the fact that Nico was Whitney's older brother. I had to kill him, and I would do anything it took to make sure that he was without life as soon as possible.

My mother came into the living room and handed Whitney a glass of apple juice, then she pulled her down onto the couch and sat beside her, taking her hand and brushing Whitney's curls from her face. "Uh, if I remember correctly, you're Nico's little sister, right? Ain't you the lil' girl he used to bring around all the time? You had those colorful barrettes in your hair with the little dresses?"

Whitney nodded. "Yes, Deb, that was me."

My mother picked up one of Whitney's arms and looked her up and down. "Damn, and this what you turned into?" She nodded and looked over to me as if to say *good job, son.* Then, she turned to the side and looked into Whitney's eyes. "You're pregnant with my grandbaby?" She asked, placing her hand on Whitney's stomach.

She nodded. "Yes, I'm about ten weeks. I love your son, Deb. I love him with all of my heart." Tears ran down her cheeks again.

My mother pulled her into her embrace and rubbed her back, frowning at me. "When were you going to tell me this, Jayden?"

I exhaled loudly. "Man, moms, let's not do this right now. I was gon' tell you after we talked about all of this other stuff. You just ain't gave me the chance to." I felt myself becoming irritated and I didn't like being that way with my mother. She was my queen, but I needed to get away from the both for a hot second. I just needed to think before I hit up the slums and got on my business. I felt like there was too much going on at one time, and I just needed to think some things over.

My mother stood up and pulled Whitney with her. "Well, obviously me and her got a bunch of catching up to do. So, I'ma take her upstairs with me, and she'll be back down later. Go ahead and get your mind together, baby. I can tell that you're frustrated."

She took a hold of Whitney's hand and led her out of the room, and as Whitney walked past me, she kissed me on the cheek, then rubbed the spot.

"I'mma go and spend some time with your mother. Please know that I love you, and I'm riding with you, against all odds. Do what you have to for our family."

* * *

That night, Whitney stayed upstairs with my mother, and I lay awake in my bed with my eyes open, thinking things over so I could develop a strategy to outsmart and ultimately kill Nico, simultaneously stacking my paper because I was still dead set on getting rich and getting the fuck up out of Philly. I had $275,000 to my name, six bricks of heroin, and five of cocaine. Though Nico was the focal point, money was definitely a close second.

At about three in the morning, there was a knock on my door, and before I could answer it, Myeesha stepped inside of the room, closed the door behind her, and locked the knob. She crept over to the bed and sat on the edge of it. She was wearing a real tiny, tight Victoria Secrets see-through, pink gown that came just below her crotch. Through the light of the moon, I could see that she wasn't wearing a bra. Both breasts were visible through the material. Her big brown nipples were erect and exposed.

She looked over to me, smiled, and rubbed my stomach. "I see you dead-set on avoiding me. What's all that about?" She whispered, running her hand up and down my stomach.

I shook my head. "I gotta figure some shit out, that's all. Once I get my mind right, I plan on spending some time with you. It's just that, right now, I'm trying to piece a bunch of things together." The scent of her perfume wafted up my nose.

exposing her big, brown nipples that seemed to always be hard.

I lifted my hips and allowed for her to pull them down my legs, leaving them along my calves. "Man, you know my girl upstairs. You on some bullshit. What if she come down here and catch us?"

Myeesha took her big titties and rubbed them all over the head of my hard dick, trapping it between the middle of them. "I don't give a fuck about her. I came up here to see you. I been thinking about you ever since we were little, and I let you take my virginity. You remember that, huh?" She leaned down and sucked me into her mouth, grabbing my dick by the base before pumping it, just like she did when we were little, and she couldn't handle all of it in her lil' mouth at one time. She swallowed me all the way down to her fist, then sucked back upward, leaving my pole leaking with her saliva. "Mmm, you like that shit?" She looked into my eyes, stroking my dick.

I shook my head. "Hell n'all. That's some lil' girl shit. You still using your hands. I ain't impressed." I grabbed her wrist and took her hand off of my pipe. "Gone, my woman do a better job than that."

She frowned and looked hurt. "I don't need to use my hands. Watch." She grabbed my dick, sucked on the head, and put her hands behind her back, sucking my pole in a slow, rhythmic motion. I watched her jaws hollow in and out. "Like that, cuz, huh?" She grabbed my hand and put it on her ass, spreading her legs further apart.

I reached across her back and slapped her cheeks, running my fingers up and down and in between her pussy's wet crease. I slid three fingers deep into her tight hole and fucking them in and out at full speed while she moaned around my dick and started to breathe harder and harder.

"Un, un, un, un, unh!"

I grabbed the back of her head. "Go all the way down. You cheatin' right now. You know the rules." I said, bringing back old memories from when we were little.

"Awww!" She moaned, then slid her lips all the way down until they were touching my pubic hairs. She gagged and kept on sucking me at full speed, while I fingered her harder and harder.

I felt my body tense up, and then all the euphoria from her sucking started to get the best of me. My eyes rolled into the back of my head, at the same time I scrunched my toes together in my ankle socks before I fell back, grabbing a handful of her long hair and coming inside her mouth while she kept on sucking me at full speed. "Huh, huh, huh, huh." I groaned cuming in large spurts.

She swallowed me, then sat back on her haunches, running her tongue over her lips. "I'm only here for a little while and I plan on playing House as much as possible." She laughed and slid two fingers into her pussy before taking them out and feeding them to me.

Chapter 4

Kilroy handed me a Tech Nine, then threw his car in drive, after covering the Mach Eleven that was in his lap with a red rag. "Bruh, I never thought it would come down to me having to kill that nigga Nico, but I ain't got a problem doing it either, especially if he crossed you and the homey Naz. Word is bond. I'd bag one of my own family for you two niggas." He turned the corner and pushed in the car lighter.

I sat back in my seat and curled my upper lip, looking out of the passenger's window to see that it was a beautiful day outside. It had to be about ninety degrees. Everywhere I looked there were women out wearing next to nothing, either pushing strollers or walking with a group of other females. I couldn't focus because they were everywhere.

I took the blunt from behind my ear, pulled out the car lighter and lit it. I took a few puffs to make sure it was good before replacing the car lighter. "Yeah, that nigga Nico done turned bitch. He fucking with them people now. I had a few detectives ride down on me and tell me everything about one of the moves that we'd pulled together. Telling me shit that only Nico would have known. On top of that, he trying to get my cousin pinched and knocked on a humbug. He threatened my moms. That nigga gotta go. It is what it is."

Kilroy was a dark skinned, heavy-set nigga with a heart of ice, and had crazy loyalty for the niggas he fucked with. My cousin Naz had introduced me to the lil' homey along with his right hand man Poppa a lil' while back. Whereas Poppa was a straight hustler and all about his dough, Kilroy was a straight head bussah. He loved to murder niggas and pull kick-doors. I'd hired him to be one of my shooters before I'd gotten knocked by the law.

I don't give a fuck how tough you were, when it came to the slums of Philly, every nigga had to have a shooter watching his back. Especially if you were knee deep in the game the way that me and Nico was. We had so many enemies that not having shooters would have been pure suicide.

Kilroy shook his head. "I don't play about my mother, kid. A muhfucka say they gon' body my ol' girl, we gon' have a problem. I'm talking about killing they whole family over one threat; newborns and all. That's word to my mother."

He beeped the horn at three thick ass, dark skinned sistas that had Daisy Dukes all up the cracks of their ass. I wished I had a horn to beep at them. They stopped in front of a cell phone shop and one of the sistas threw their arms into the air, and yelled, "What's good?"

I smiled and nodded. "That's what I'm thinking. That nigga Nico gotta got to sleep indefinitely before we start bringing family into this shit. I ain't ever been that type to prey on a nigga's family. I prefer to go straight at his chin, nah'mean?"

I frowned as I watched Kilroy pulling up alongside the dark skinned sista that had thrown her arms in the air. Now that we were close enough, I could really make out just how strapped and fine she was. I was impressed, yet still a little thrown off because Kilroy had pulled up alongside them.

"What you on, kid?"

He smiled and threw his car in park. "Yo, I love dark skinned hoes, son. I gotta see what's good with shorty right here, then we can rollout to the trap. I got some new shit I wanna show you anyway, plus that nigga Poppa wanna sit down with you and make a few propositions that I think might be right up your alley. Kid getting money now." He said, opening his car door and getting out. He walked around the front of the car while the sun shined in through his windshield. Before he could make it halfway to the females, they surrounded him, and all got to trying to talk to him at once. He started to hug one at a time, grabbing their fat asses and laughing.

I looked down at my phone as it vibrated with a text coming through from Myeesha, saying that she couldn't wait until tonight, whatever that meant. I could already see that she was going to be a problem. I didn't know what my mother would say if she found out that we were playing around the way that we were, even though we had been doing it ever since we were little kids. I guessed old habits died harder than I thought.

I honestly couldn't believe how bad Myeesha had gotten. It was one of the reasons it was so hard to turn her ass down, even though I honestly did not want to hurt Whitney. I just felt like I didn't have that much dick control. If a chick was fine, strapped as hell, and ready to go, I was more than likely going, even if I knew I shouldn't. I didn't understand that about myself, and at that time I didn't feel like I had to. I was young and in the streets. Unconditional love and faithfulness would come later, I guessed.

Kilroy put about three of the females' numbers into his phone before hugging them and watching them walk off, switching harder than they had been before. Their tiny shorts were all in their asses, leaving their chocolate cheeks exposed and jiggling as they walked away. I understood fully why he had to jump out of the car. Had Myeesha not worked on me all night, I probably would have been out there with him just as thirsty.

He got into the car and slammed the door, reached under his seat and placed the Mach Eleven back onto his lap, covering it once again with a red rag. "Kid, that was my fault. I'm ready to roll out now. My night gon' be set. Them lil' hoes are sisters, and two of them talking like they cool with a threesome tonight, so you know I gotta see what's really good. I'm trying to catch a cavity with all that chocolate." He laughed, started the car and pulled off into traffic. "How you wanna handle Nico ass?"

I sat back in my seat and looked around outside before trailing my eyes down to his dashboard and seeing that his tank was well below the empty point. "Say, kid, you gotta stop and get some gas or we about to be stranded out here. You see that?" I asked, tapping the dashboard.

He frowned, then looked down. "Damn. I don't know how I missed that shit. I gotta quit fucking with that Lean 'cause it's causing me to lose myself a lil'." He shook his head. "It's cool. We can pull into this BP up the street and fill my tank up. I need to grab a couple snacks anyway. I'm hungry as a muthafucka." He stepped on the gas.

"Far as this Nico situation go, I'm trying to get at kid right away. That way we can get back to the money. It's a reason I'm hittin' you up before I even hollered at Naz about this. I know you'll handle that business and son will be on his way before I know it."

Kilroy looked in his rear-view mirror and scrunched his face. "Yo, why this nigga riding my bumper, son? Fuck is his problem?" He looked over his shoulder and mugged the money green Benz truck behind us, before slowly pulling into the BP gas station right up to a pump.

As soon as he stepped on the brakes and threw the car in park, I noticed the doors of the truck behind us open. About four niggas jumped out of it and rushed our car with their hands under their shirts. Kilroy threw the rag off his Mach Eleven immediately and cocked it back. I did the same with my Tech, ready to air their asses out.

One of them stopped about halfway to Kilroy's open window and called his name. "Kilroy! Kilroy! This ain't got nothin' to do with you, man. We trying to get at that nigga in yo' passenger's seat. Son ran in our trap, so fall back!"

Kilroy stuck his head out of the window and mugged them. "This my nigga, Pablo, and what the fuck you doing riding up on me like that? I thought we had an agreement!" Kilroy said, opening his car door and facing him with the Mach Eleven aimed in his direction. "Tell yo' niggas to get they bitch ass back in the truck or we about to light this muhfucka up. Then you come holler at me like a man. Do it!"

He hollered with his finger wavering on the trigger of his gun.

I watched Pablo say something to his crew in Spanish before they began to slowly retreat to the truck. Then, he turned to Kilroy with a mug on his face. "Let me holler at you, Kilroy, because I ain't trying to kick off a new war between the Shooters and my Posse. All of this can be squashed if you'll let me get at this nigga that ran in my trap, or he give me my shit back."

I was squinting, trying to see if I remembered him from anywhere and I didn't. Me and Nico had robbed so many niggas that I didn't know if I could place half of their faces. "Yo, fuck that nigga, Kilroy. Word is bond. If you don't pull off, I'm finna wet this nigga." I said, curling my upper lip, preparing to hop into the backseat so I could get a better shot at him and his crew.

"Pablo, who told you that bullshit about my nigga? I know he don't get down like that." Kilroy said, easing further out of the car until half of his body was out of it, though his Mach was still hidden inside of it.

Pablo came closer. "That fool Nico told us everything. I know that's Jayden in there, and I know that Jazz gave him the low down on my trap. I don't wanna play all these games. He's either gon' give me my shit back, and I'll excuse him and say he didn't know he was robbing the Mexican Posse, or he can keep that shit, and sooner or later we'll catch up with him and fuck him over when you aren't around. Either way, somebody gon' pay for what took place."

I looked all around and saw cars pulling in and out of the gas station, going on about their lives as if nothing was taking place out of the ordinary. I didn't think they had a clue that bullets were about to be flying real soon.

Kilroy scrunched his face harder. "That nigga Nico lying. Like I said, my nigga don't get down like that, and furthermore, he plugged with the Shooters, so if you beefing with him, you beefing with us." Kilroy leaned all the way out of the car, aimed and let his Mach Eleven ride.

Boom-boom-boom! Boom-boom-boom! The Mach jumped in his hand again and again. His bullets slammed into Pablo's chest and knocked the man backward, causing him to fall into the hood of his money green Benz truck. I opened the passenger's door and started to chop the truck down. *Bock-bock-bock-bock-bock-bock!* My bullets flew into the windshield, shattering it, while the other bullets implanted themselves in the truck's exterior. One of the dudes jumped behind the wheel and tried to back it out of the gas station, but only managed to crash it into a car full of females. I could hear them screaming at the top of their lungs.

Kilroy jumped back into the car and threw it in drive. "Let's go, nigga, fuck them. We'll finish them off at another time."

I sat back in the passenger's seat just as he shot out of the gas station at full speed with the tires burning rubber.

* * *

An hour later, I finished pouring gasoline all over the car's interior before Kilroy lit a match and jumped back. Flames shot all through it before the entire car was ignited.

Naz paced with a cigarette in his hand. "What the fuck is wrong with that nigga, son? Kid snitching to them people and our enemies. What type of shit is that?"

The car began to crackle inside of the filthy warehouse that had once been a glass factory. I could barely think straight. I didn't know what Nico had on his brain because he was doing shit that I never thought he'd ever do. Snitching was a cardinal sin for us. Back in the day, we often said that we'd rather die than to ever snitch on another nigga, and I guess in that moment I was wondering what happened to Nico's street morals?

Poppa put his arm around my shoulder as the heat from the car began to warm my skin. "Yo, I know you hurt, Jayden, but I just want you to know that we got you. If anybody want it with you, then they want it with the Shooters. We got niggas out scouring the city right now looking for Nico, so it's only a matter of time. Trust me on that." His eyes got bucked, then he was pulling me backward. "Yo, that bitch about to blow."

We jogged until we were standing outside of the warehouse, just as the car crackled, and then blew up with fire coming from it.

I found myself back at Poppa's trap twenty minutes later, sitting on a couch beside Naz and Kilroy, with Poppa sitting across from us with a mug on his face. He took his two pistols off of his waist and set them on the table, just as Kilroy jumped up and turned off the television that we'd been watching with the sound off. The shooting was all over the news. Pablo had been murdered and two members of his crew had been wounded. The media was saying it was a gang hit, while witnesses said it was an attempted robbery. At the time, they didn't have any suspects, though they did say that the authorities would be reviewing the footage from the security camera.

Kilroy shook his head. "That Nico gotta die, kid. This muhfucka got us beefing with them Essays." He shook his head again and rubbed his temples.

Naz stood up and shrugged. "Fuck them Spicks. It is what it is. They want a war, then that's what we gon' bring to them, and I say we go at them first because once they come, they ain't gon' stop. We gotta make a statement right away, nah'mean? Kilroy you gotta get the shooters ready to handle business. Meanwhile, Poppa, you gotta relocate for a minute, and you and Jayden need to roll up to DC and get money for like a month straight. That way we'll keep our chips in order. Me and Kilroy will handle shit back here until then. I'm thinking we put twenty gees on Nico's head. That way the streets'll more than likely do our job for us. What you think, Jayden?"

"I got that put up, so that sound good. But what's up with DC? Who we know out there?" I asked, confused because this was the first time I was hearing about going out that way. Me and Nico had robbed a few niggas in DC some years back, and that was the only dealings I'd ever had with that city.

Poppa put his pistols back on his hip. "Yo, since you been on lock, I been fucking around out there after my sister's baby's daddy got knocked by the feds. He left her some nice pieces of dog food to work with. I used the birds that you left me and some of the shit from what she gave me, went out there and been making a killing ever since. We trap on a set full of Treetop Bloodz. They just moved out that way from Virginia. My uncle calling for them, so it's good. It's about fifteen of the shooters already out there getting money for us, so all we gotta do is re-up on our work and get out there. It's money galore, trust me." He said, tightening his belt. "We got two apartment buildings on Jackson Drive. One for heroin and one for crack. Both bitches are booming and protected by the Bloodz and our Shooters. I say we rush out there and go back to eating. Time is money, and we gon' need it since we are entering into a new war with the Mexican Posse."

I shrugged. "I'm with it. I got a few birds at the crib I need to snatch up. After that, it's good." I turned to Kilroy. "Yo, you sure y'all don't want me to stay in town and go at them Mexicans with you? I mean, after all, all of this shit is because of me, and I can handle my own if need be."

Kilroy waved me off and shook his head. "N'all, son, it ain't even about that. I get bored with all this trapping and shit. I need to keep some blood on my hands in order to stay awake, so do the homey Naz." He laughed and looked over to Naz who smiled, and sat down on the couch, sliding an AR-15 from underneath it and rubbing along its side. "Poppa get how we get down, and you should too. It's two parts of the Shooters. One side hustle like crazy, and the other side lay niggas down and cause a whole lot of funerals. You know, keep Mr. Jones over at the Funeral Home in business." He laughed again. "Both sides of the mob are needed. Then, on top of that, Nico bitch ass tried to get the homey pinched. We can't take that shit lying down. Naz is like my pops, man. I love this dude, so my loyalty to him is lethal. I gotta be the one to put that bullet in Nico's head, and in the meantime, I never liked Pablo and his crew of Mexicans. Them niggas are more racist than white supremacists. It's long overdue for what they got coming." He scrunched his face. "Long story short, if we need you niggas, we'll give you a holler. When we close in on Nico, Jayden, you'll be the first to know. Until then, y'all go and get money so our mob can be strengthened, even in times of warfare."

Naz nodded. "Yeah, we got this, lil' cuz. Leave this animal shit to us savages."

I ain't know what he meant by that saying, but I didn't feel like arguing with him, so I didn't say shit.

* * *

That night, I went to my mother's house and loaded up four kilos of dope. I took two of heroin and two of cocaine and placed them in my duffle bag. Afterward, I showered, getting myself together. I was on my way out of the house when my mother, Whitney and Myeesha came into the crib with a bunch of grocery bags from Walmart. I had it in my mind to brush pass them and keep it moving, but Whitney blocked my path, holding a big brown paper bag in her arms that was filled with groceries.

"Baby, can I talk to you for a minute?" she asked, looking me over.

I nodded and moved to the side so my mother and cousin could get past, then stepped out onto the porch with her. She'd sat the grocery bag on the living room table, then stepped out with me, rubbing her shoulders because it was very windy outside.

"What's good, baby?" I asked, ready to get a move on.

She grabbed my wrist and looked into my eyes. "Jayden, my cousins are here from New York. Nico called them in so they can hunt you down and kill you. They're more than twenty-deep, Bronx Crips, and they are just as crazy as you and Nico. I'm so scared for you that I don't know what to do." She said looking up at me with watery eyes.

I shrugged. "Fuck Nico. I ain't worried about him or your cousins. If them niggas want war, then let's do it. I'll meet that nigga anywhere he want to, long as he show up."

She tightened her grip on my wrist. "Jayden, we have a baby on the way. There is no time for you to be out here warring with my brother, who is going to be our child's uncle. Now, I need for you guys to squash this beef or things are going to get ugly. My cousins are relentless. Haven't you ever heard of the Bronx Crips?"

I yanked my wrist away from her because I felt like she thought I should bow down because of how crazy her cousins were supposed to be, when, I didn't give a fuck about none of them niggas, even though I knew how they got down. "Let me go, Whitney. I don't care how crazy yo' people is. I don't fear them or Nico. They gotta do what they gotta do, and so do I."

I started to walk down the steps when Myeesha shot out of the house, ran to my car and got in.

Whitney's eyes lowered in anger, then she looked up to me. "Well, Deb has invited me to stay here with her, and I think it's in my best interest to do so. I don't think Nico would try and attack her as long as I am here, so this is where I'm going to be until you two grow up. Deb is going to go to the doctor with me later. I've been feeling a little off and I just want to make sure everything is good with our unborn child. Emphasis on *ours*." She exhaled loudly. "I love you, Jayden. Always have and always will. I need for you to let this thing go so that you can become the father that I'm going to need for our child." She stepped on her tippy toes and kissed my cheek before looking over her shoulder at my car and shaking her head. "I guess she going with you, wherever that is." She stepped into the house and closed the door behind her.

Ghost

Chapter 5

It didn't matter how much I argued with Myeesha, she refused to get out of my car. Even when I threatened to whoop her ass, though I knew I never would have. So, anyway, she wound up rolling out to DC with me, swearing that no matter what went down she wasn't going to leave my side.

We got there at about six at night. I met up with Poppa on Jackson Drive. I simply parked my car at the corner and had to call him to be escorted into the Bloods hood because, when I pulled up, there were about fifty niggas all over that block with red shirts on, red bandanas around their necks, red flags hanging out of their pockets and around their hands. I'd never seen so many Bloods in one place at one time. And all of them niggas looked grimy as hell. They mugged the fuck out of my car, all the way up until Poppa came strolling down the block with ten of the Shooters. Only then, did he wave for me to drive down the block and I did, though on high alert.

Myeesha's eyes were wide open. "Damn, maybe I didn't know what I was getting into." She said, looking all around outside with her fingernail in her mouth.

I grabbed her waist and made her sit down. "You good, cuz. You with me and I ain't gon' let shit happen to you." I said, sounding tougher than I felt because I was thinking I'd made the wrong decision traveling to DC when I didn't know nobody out there other than Poppa.

Poppa directed me into a parking lot and then guided me to follow him all the way into the back of it while he walked along side of my whip.

After I found a parking spot, I saw that the parking lot was filled with his Shooters from Philly, so I got out and gave him a half of hug. "What it do, kid?" I asked.

He hugged me back and then looked down and into my car. "Who is shorty right there?" He licked his lips and nodded.

I pulled him up. "That's my cousin right there. She heard about all that dumb shit with Nico and decided she wasn't gon' leave my side. I ain't feel like arguing, so she gon' be with me while I'm up here this time. That cool?"

Poppa shrugged. "It's a lil' different, but it's good. What's her name?"

"Myeesha, and hands off, lil' nigga. This my blood, and I'll clap a nigga quick over her."

Poppa laughed. "Whoa, whoa, whoa, aiight, nigga. Point taken. Come on, let's get inside and get this work whipped up, so we can hit the ground running." He waved for me to follow him.

I reached into the backseat and grabbed my duffle bag of product, then closed it back. Then, I walked around and opened Myeesha's door just as about ten Bloods came into the parking lot with their shirts off and guns in their waistbands.

There was one in particular, a dark-skinned, tall, skinny nigga, with long ass dreads, who had five-point stars all over his chest that walked up to Poppa and pointed at me. "Who is he, Blood?"

Poppa looked him in the eyes and curled his upper lip. "That's my mans right there. He from Philly, and we trapping together."

The dark-skinned dude nodded and looked me over. "Kid got on a whole lot of blue. Fuck is he, Cuzz or somethin'? If so, I don't know about this G-pass. It's enough Opps in your crew already." He placed his hand on the handle of his Forty-Five and mugged me to death, sucking his teeth loudly.

I ushered Myeesha back into the car and told her to chill, before I walked over to him as his troops surrounded me with their hands on their weapons. I stepped a foot away from his face. The handle of my Uzi clearly poked out of my waistband. "Bruh, I don't roll Cuzz or Blood. I get money with the Shooters, so it's good. I ain't got no beef with you niggas, and never have."

He sucked his teeth and looked me up and down before smiling, exposing a mouth full of gold. It seemed to shine even harder because he was so black. He looked around at his crew as they closed in on me. "Yeah, well, aiight then. Seeing as the homey right here got asylum with us Bloods, I guess since you're in his entourage, you get diplomatic immunity. You lucky, too. Last nigga walked up on me is headless now." He laughed and waved for his troops to file out of the parking lot.

I saw that his back was tatted with the state of Virginia and had five-point stars everywhere. I'd never been to Virginia before, but I got the impression that them niggas got down because they had fully taken over that hood. Everywhere I looked

I saw red, or a nigga with a pistol and a mug on his face.

Poppa mugged their whole crew until they were out of the parking lot. "Word is bond, kid, we gon' take over this whole area real soon. Them Blood niggas living on borrowed time. This shit gon' belong to the Shooters." He blew air through his teeth and walked toward the building.

I got Myeesha out of the car and we followed him inside. As soon as I got inside of the hallway, I could smell the strong scent of crack cocaine. I could tell that somebody was cooking up a nice batch.

Poppa looked over his shoulder at me and smiled. "That's that Columbian Mayonnaise that's being whipped. Got a plug on them chickens from out of Yonkers. Twelve a kilo. My uncle put me in, but you'll find out about all that later. For now, we gon' head upstairs and buss your bricks down and get shit popping. Shop will be back open in two hours and the feens gon' rush us like its Black Friday."

* * *

Ninety minutes later, I'd cooked up a half of a kilo while the Shooters broke it down and bagged up all dimes. Meanwhile, my cousin Myeesha and three of the Shooters sat at another table foiling up a half kilo of heroin, right before Poppa opened up shop. Shit got crazy right away. I looked out the window and saw that there was a long line in the back of the parking lot, where I'd parked my car, and the line was full of nothing but dope fiends. I couldn't believe it.

The Shooters kept on running in and out of our apartment, grabbing quantities of dope before heading back out and serving the hypes. Then, they'd comeback with a bundle of money and hand it to either me or Poppa. Poppa had two safes in the trap that he gave me the combinations to, so every thousand dollars I'd place the money into one of the safes before locking it back. We got down like this the entire night, all the way until two in the morning, when we shut down shop for the night.

Poppa came to me and gave me a half of hug. "Yo, you see how we ran through two birds in one day? Nigga, it's money to be got out here in DC. I'm ready to run them Blood niggas off so we can get all of the cash. Damn my uncle." He laughed.

Myeesha got up from the couch to come and lay her head on my chest. "I'm tired, Jayden. Where we about to sleep at, 'cause I know it can't be here?" She asked, looking around at the house full of niggas that had pistols on their waists and blunts in their mouths. I could tell that she was extremely uncomfortable.

I put my arm around her and looked down at Poppa. "Where you sleep at, kid?" I yawned, and covered my mouth with my fist.

He laughed and waved his hand around the apartment. "I'm a trap nigga. I sleep in either one of the rooms in this building, or the one next door. But it don't bother me." He shook his head. "I can see why it would her though because she's a female and it's a few of the homeys that's been giving shorty lil' thick ass the eye, including myself. So, if I was you I'd take her to the Ramada Inn up the street so she can get some rest. You look like you need some too, bruh. No offense."

I yawned again and covered my mouth the same way. "None taken. Yeah, I guess that's what I'ma do. I'll hit you up in the morning and we'll get right back to it, first thing. Love, fool." I gave him a half of hug, and made my way toward the front door with my arms around Myeesha's waist. I looked back to see Poppa looking down at her ass, biting on his bottom lip and shaking his head. "Aiight, nigga, I done told you about her. I'm serious." I said, feeling my heartrate speed up.

Poppa laughed and didn't take his eyes off of Myeesha's ass that was encased in some tight Fendi pants that left little to the imagination. "Yo, I'm just looking. I ain't ever seen a mixed chick so strapped before. I'll give your cousin ten bands right now to spend a night with me. Word is bond."

I released Myeesha and turned to face him with my face balled up. I was ready to snatch his lil' skinny ass up and drop him on his head. I was sleepy, a lil' cranky, and tired of him coming at my cousin like I wasn't standing right there, but before I could snap, he raised his hands in the air and started laughing like the shit was funny.

"Yo, I'm just fucking with you, but she is bad though. Come on, let me escort y'all out of the hood so them Blood niggas won't try no bullshit."

* * *

I took my shirt off and placed it on the chair beside the hotel bed. Then, I stretched my arms above my head, and yawned loudly. The bathroom door opened, and Myeesha stepped out of it wearing some tight, purple Victoria's Secret bikini cut panties that were all up in her pussy lips. From where she stood, I could see a bald golden sex lip on each side of her crotch band. She also had on a small tank top that stopped just below her titties. Both of her nipples poked through the material.

She rubbed the front of her panties and ran her tongue across her lips. "You acted like you was gon' tear your guy head off over me. Do you have any idea how that made me feel?" She asked as she walked over to me and stood between my legs.

I rubbed all over them thick ass cheeks. I squeezed them and smacked them just enough to make them jiggle. "When have I ever played about you? You remember when we were little, I knocked your so-called boyfriend out for calling you a bitch. You know what it is." I spread them ass cheeks and ran my finger up and down her crease, feeling the thong that was all up in her ass.

She laughed and placed her hands on my shoulders, leaning down and kissing my lips. "I remember his whole family jumped on you, and then later that day you popped his ass. You ain't been back in Atlanta since then." She licked my lips, then sucked them into her mouth, moaning passionately.

I kissed her back, hard, then broke it. "Turn around and back up. Let me eat that pussy and that ass from the back. I feel like I need to taste you, bad. For some reason, seeing all them niggas fawning all over you all day got me feeling some type of way." I licked her stomach and turned her around.

She bent over and backed into my face. My nose went right up her ass crack. I yanked her panties to the side and licked her slit, holding her hips before going to town like I was starving for that forbidden body.

She reached behind herself and pulled her ass cheeks apart. "Unnn, yes, eat me, Jayden. Unn, just like you used to when we were little and played hide and seek. Unnn, you remember that?"

I pinched her clit and drove my tongue in and out of her back door before sucking on her clit and licking her slit. Up and down, side to side, I kept going with her ass cheeks on my face.

She reached under herself and played with her pussy. "I want you to fuck me so bad, Jayden. Unnn! I need you to fuck me. Please, cuz. Please give me some dick. I'm begging you!" She hollered.

I was sucking all over her ass cheeks by this point, while playing with her clitoris, pinching it, sending chills through her body.

"Unn! Uhh! Please, yes! Yes!" She spread her legs wider apart. I turned my head sideways, trapping both of her pussy lips, then ran my tongue in and out of her. "Fuck this shit, Jayden. Fuck this! I want some dick." She stood up and laid in bed on her back, pulling her panties to the side and rubbing her pussy in crazy circles. "Let me see your dick, Jayden, before you fuck me. Let me see you stroke it like when we were little, and I was scared of it. I just wanna be a lil' girl again." She arched her back and slid two fingers into herself. "Unnn, please, let me see it."

I dropped my pants and boxers, then stood before her with my dick throbbing like crazy. I looked between her legs and saw how fat her naked pussy was, with the way its lips opened to reveal her pink insides, and saw the juice coming from out of her hole. I couldn't help stroking my dick. "Unn, I'm finna kill that pussy, Myeesha. You know it, too." I said, watching her finger herself faster and faster while her eyes stayed pinned on my pipe.

She'd take her two fingers and open her lips real wide, then smash them together while her fingers on her right hand shot in and out of her. Her thumb assaulted her clit in mad circles. "Unn, unn. You. Gon'. Fuck me like when we were little? Huh, Jayden?" She raised her ass from the bed and opened her thick thighs wider. Her toes curled before she straightened them all over again, and still her eyes never left the sights of my dick. I could tell that she wanted it bad.

I got on the bed, right between her legs, leaned down and licked all over her pussy coated fingers; sucking on her wrist while she continued to dig deep within her womb. Tasting her salt, I loved it. "I want this pussy, Myeesha. I'm gon' hurt this shit. I promise you that."

I yanked her hand out of the way and sucked her clit into my mouth again, nipping at it with my teeth, while she reached under me and took a hold of my dick, pulling on it.

"Mmm-a! I want this dick, cuz! Please! Gimme this dick, now!" She whimpered, opening her thighs wider, allowing for me to swallow her running juices. She was all over my lips and chin. I could taste her heavily on my tongue.

I stood on my knees and pushed her down to the bed, sucking and biting on her neck hard while she moaned in my ear and tried to pull me on top of her. I wiggled out of her embrace and tore her panties from her frame, then pulled her shirt up to expose her pretty titties with the huge nipples. Squeezing her breasts together, I sucked first one nipple and then the other, pulling on them with my teeth.

"Ahhh! Shit! Please, hurry! Fuck me, Jayden. I can't take it no more. I need this dick." She said, reaching between us and trying to force my dick into her little hole.

Every time the head went into her crease, I turned my hips to make it fall back out. I knew the more I teased her, the wetter she would become. I thought about all of the hide and seek games we played when we were little. She'd always hide in a spot that she knew I'd find her, and once I did, I'd pull up her little dress while she laid on her back, get between her legs and hump into her center while she held my waist. It was how it all started. Now she was a grown woman— fine and thick as hell— ready to go. I couldn't wait to be inside of her body.

She sat up and kissed all over my lips; licking them and moaning into my face. "Do me, cuz. Please, I wanna feel you inside of me right now. I'm begging you." She laid on her back again, spreading her legs wide. Pussy juices ran out of her lips and oozed down her thick ass cheeks. Her scent was heavy in the room already, intoxicating me on so many levels.

"Aiight, I'm finna fuck this pussy on some grown man shit then. Let's get it."

I picked up her left thick thigh, put it up against my chest while I placed my dick head on her pussy

she arched her back while I pounded her out and sped up the pace.

Now I was going so fast that it sounded like the bed was trying to come through the wall. The springs were so loud that it sounded like we were jumping up and down in the bed like little kids, instead of fucking like we were.

My eyes rolled into the back of my head, then I looked down again and saw how my pipe looked going in and out of her pussy. Every time I slammed forward, her sex lips would smash together, and when I pulled backward they would open up widely and leave my dick coated in her cream. I started to think about who she was and our relation to each other, and it was too much for me to handle. I folded her into a ball, slamming my dick into her. I got about forty more strokes in before I was coming deep within her channel, feeling her nails scratch all over my lower back, but it didn't stop me from plunging forward harder and harder while my nut shot into her.

"Uhh! Uh! Uhh! I feel it. I feel it. Ummm, yes," were her last word before we spent the next five minutes kissing and sucking allover each other's bodies. We couldn't get enough.

She broke our embrace, took my dick and sucked him into her mouth, licking her juices off of it loudly. "We taste good together." More sucking. "Umm, we taste so good together, Jayden." She licked up and down it while I rubbed and squeezed her fat ass.

I wanted to hit that muhfucka, and I knew that before she went back to Atlanta that I would. I didn't give a fuck what took place. I had to.

She sucked me for another five minutes, then climbed up my body, took my hard dick and slid it back into her. "Ummm, Jayden." Then, she laid her head on my chest, riding me real slow and sensual.

I gripped that fat ass booty with both hands with one on each cheek, guiding her up and down my mans. "I love this pussy, Myeesha. You hear me? I love this shit." I said, rubbing into her ass crack.

She sat up and looked down on me, with both of her titties jiggling. "Mmm, its yours, Jayden. It always have been. You just never came back to the A. Unnn, this big ass dick." She leaned forward then popped her back slowly. "I missed you. I swear, I missed you so much." She laid her head back on to my chest, licking my nipple before hugging me and stopping her riding of my pipe. "Can you hold me for the rest of the night? I really need to be held by you." She disconnected our sexes and laid on her side, pulling my arm around her.

We spooned and I kissed the back of her neck. I loved doing that to a female when I held them, especially after fucking because all of their scent wafted from their scalps and went right up my nostrils. There was nothing like the scent of a woman. It was my weakness.

I kissed her neck again and held her more firmly. "I wish you ain't have to leave and go back down there. I'd make sure you were good if you stayed up here with me. That's my word." I kissed her again and humped into her ass.

She pushed backward and exhaled loudly. "I'd love to stay up here with you, Jayden, but you got a lot going on. You barely have any time for me right now. What would you do if I did stay? What about Whitney? Ain't y'all about to have a baby and all that?" She asked, trying to look back at me. "I'm already jealous over that shit. You know I'll become a problem real quick. I don't care what our relation is, when I'm around you I feel like I own yo' ass. Ain't shit changed. I'm still crazy." She laughed and laid her head backward.

I reached around and cuffed her right breast, running my thumb across her erect nipple. "Like I said, if you stayed up here with me, I'd make sure you were good. Take that how you want to. Ain't nothing like this forbidden body right here. You know how we get down."

She rubbed her ass in my lap and giggled. "Yeah, I guess you right, 'cause when you were in me all I kept thinking about is who you are, and it got me wetter and wetter. I know I got issues." She raised her leg as she felt me searching with my dick head for her hole again.

I slid easily into her hole and slammed forward. "Yeah, you and me both."

Chapter 6

"These are M-Fours. Fully automatic assault rifles that hold thirty in the clip and will empty the whole magazine in three seconds. On top of that, these bitches are accurate. I can hit a nigga from a half a block away and knock a hole through his ass with no remorse. The Ricans want five gees a piece for each one, but I say we set up a meeting and rob they ass for all of them and get 'em for free. That way we save money, and we'll have the weaponry to get at them, Nico, and Pablo's people. Fuck ducking any action, it's time to go hard." Kilroy said, before tooting up a thick line of cocaine, after handing me the M-4 to look it over.

Pappa sat on the couch with a fist full of $100 bills, counting them one at a time, licking his finger between every five or so. "Yo, Jayden, usually I don't like to create new drama with niggas, but these Ricans sweet as hell. They ain't got no killas standing behind them, and they getting these tools from some white boys that got a plug with the National Guard. Long story short, if we hit them, we can get them rifles and whatever else they got on hand. We at war with a few crews, plus, I'm hearing that Nico plugged in with them C's from the Bronx. Ain't no telling what they holding, and it's only a matter of time before we have to go at them toe to toe, or weapon for weapon. That includes the Mexican Posse." He put a stack of hundreds on the table and reached for the M-4.

I handed it to him and took the blunt out of the ashtray to pull off of it. We were inside one of the buildings in DC. We'd been trapping for two days straight when Kilroy showed up with the M-4 and the proposition. I sat back on the couch and nodded. "Yo, if y'all think it's a good move, then I trust you. Y'all my lil' niggas, and we in this shit together. I say we handle this business, then take a good look at the Mexican Posse over on Chambers Street. That's where they are the strongest. If we hit a couple of their traps to let 'em know we ain't playing, I'm sure they gon' lay they ass down."

Kilroy pulled on his nose and licked his lips. "Yo, if we gon' move on these M-Fours, then we gotta do this shit tomorrow night. I'll have Roberto set the shit up. He's the one that put me up on the move. He good people, and I know where his whole family resides, so we ain't gotta worry about him being on no dumb shit." Kilroy sniffled loudly and pulled his nose again. "I'll get shit together and we'll go from there. It's that the Shooters have some shit that we can make some noise with, nah'mean?" He separated four more lines of coke and tooted up a thick line, coughed and sucked his teeth loudly.

Poppa took a bundle of hundreds, folded them and handed them to me. "Here, Boss, this ten gees right here. It's yours. Mine over here, and this is yours, Kilroy." He handed him a bundle of hundreds.

Kilroy took the money and placed it in his lap. "Good looking, kid. Gotta make sure my baby mother straight. I been in the streets so much I ain't been home in a few. Yo, Jayden, you remember them dark skinned bitches from the other day?" He asked, preparing his next line to toot, pulling on his nose.

I nodded. "Yeah, son, what about 'em?" I put my bread in my pocket. I would have to check on my mother's bills and make sure Shawn was straight. Shawn was Naz's baby mother. A female I'd grown up with. My cousin Naz had a tendency to neglect her and their son, so I took it upon myself to always make sure that she was good and in a good place.

Kilroy smiled. "Yo, I wound up fucking two of the sisters together. Then, we got caught by their mother, and I expected shorty to snap out or try and kill me or something for fucking her daughters, especially at the same time. Trust me, I had them doing some shit to each other that would blow your mind. But anyway, instead of her losing it, kid, this bitch kick them out and wound up fucking me senseless. I found out all of them are Jamaican, and apparently that ain't the first time they got down like that. I feel like I wanna move in with they ass. Word is bond. You should've been there." He leaned down and tooted up his dope again.

Poppa shook his head. "Yo, that shit sound sick to me. But I guess." He started to count his money again.

I wanted to congratulate Kilroy. Instead, I kept my comments to myself and tried to get my mind right for the lick we were about to hit.

* * *

Later that night, I met up with Whitney right outside of a Philly Mom and Pop diner by the name of Chlora's. Chlora's was a small restaurant that was famous for their cheese burgers, and their biggest clientele were truckers who drove in and out of

Pennsylvania. When I walked into the restaurant, she was seated all the way in the back of it, in a booth. She had a Gucci headscarf around her head, and a big pair of Nine West sunglasses, sipping on apple juice. When she saw me, she didn't even stand up to greet me. I found that odd, and it hurt my feelings a lil' bit, even though I didn't really know why. But instead of making a big deal of it, I simply slid into the booth across from her just as a blonde waitress walked over with a pen and writing pad in her hand.

"Hello. How are you doing? Can I take your order?" She asked before adjusting her glasses on her big nose.

I nodded. "Yeah." I looked across the table at Whitney. "Do you want anything?"

She looked up to the waitress. "I'll have a cheeseburger and a medium order of steak fries, please."

The waitress wrote down her order. "Is that all?" She asked, looking down at her notepad.

"That, and another glass of apple juice, please and thank you."

The waitress nodded once again, then looked down at me. "And for you, sir? What would you like?"

"I'd like the same thing she ordered, but can you make sure that my burger is well done? I don't wanna see no pink or blood. Ugh. I want my food cooked through and through. And I'll take a cranberry juice instead of apple. Appreciate that."

She laughed and shook her head. "Okay, I'll make sure that our chef knows this. Until then, you guys enjoy yourselves, and if you need anything, don't hesitate to call me over." She put her pen behind her ear and walked to the next table and took their order with a big smile across her face.

Whitney exhaled and looked across the table at me. "So, how are you?" She took her glasses off and set them on the table.

I nonchalantly adjusted the Forty-Five in my waistband because the handle was sticking me in the ribs. "I'm good. I'm just a little worried about you. How is our baby doing?" I asked, reaching across the table and touching her hand.

She pulled it back and placed it inside her lap. "Our child is coming along just fine. I wish that it would have been you beside me for our doctor's appointment and not your mother, but it was what it was. I just hope that this isn't a glimpse into our future because if so, I don't know if I'm strong enough to sustain this. I needed you there, Jayden. I didn't know what to expect. You were supposed to be right there beside me through the whole process. Instead, you were out in the streets doing only God knows what. It hurts." She lowered her head and took another deep breath, blowing it out very slowly.

I felt like crap because everything she had said was exactly right. I should have been there beside her and there was no excuse for me not being there. I shook my head and reached across the table once again to take her hand into my own. This time she allowed for me to grab and hold it. "I'm sorry, baby. You're right. I should have been there because there is nothing more important than you and our child. You shouldn't have had to be there on your own, and I already know that my mother is no proper substitute for me. I'm sorry, and I can admit that I was out of line. Can you please forgive me?" I asked, looking into her pretty eyes.

She flipped her long, curly hair over her shoulders and looked off into the distance, refusing to make eye contact with me. "You know, I knew I was out of order to cross the line with you in the first place, Jayden, but I thought that if any man was worth breaking promises to my brother, it was you. A man that had been there every step of the way. Always protected me, and made sure that I was all good, even when my brother was there and in the picture. You always catered to me, but it's like now that I'm pregnant, you're doing everything but the right thing, and you're not understanding that this is the time that I need you the most because I'm losing my freaking mind trying to figure everything out." She lowered her head and exhaled loudly before tilting it backward and opening her eyes wide so she wouldn't cry.

Seeing her in that vulnerable state of mind really hurt my heart, especially because I knew that I was the cause of it. I had to do better. I had to find a way to cater to her emotions more. To make her feel more of a priority of mine. I shook my head and squeezed her hand. "Baby, what do you want me to do? How can I be the best man for you during this pregnancy? I'll do anything. Just say it." I felt my throat getting tight because I never wanted to be the one to hurt Whitney. I truly loved and cared about her with all of my heart. I knew that may not have seemed like the truth, but it really was. I'd always loved her.

She shrugged. "Jayden, I can't expect you to be more than what you are. I mean, for as long as I've known you, you've always been in the streets and running from here and there, and wherever you wanted to. I can't expect you to change just because we're having a baby. I'm not that stupid."

I ran my hand over my face and exhaled loudly. I was getting a little irritated because it felt like I was going to have to beg her to tell me what she expected for me to be doing, even though I guess I should have already known. Believe it or not, I was still immature to things like this.

"Why are you getting irritated right now?" She asked, taking her hand away and hugging herself. She hook her head. "This is why I didn't want to say anything. I haven't seen you in a few days and I didn't want to argue. I just wanted to spend some time with you before we went our separate ways. I still love you a lot. I'm just going through something right now. That's all." She blinked, and tears ran out of her eyes.

I looked across the table at her before getting up and sliding around to her side. Placing my arm around her shoulder, I kissed the side of her forehead. "Baby, I'm sorry, but you know that things are crazy right now. We can't kick it the way we want because I'm beefing with Nico. That issue has to be resolved, and I can't let me guards down, you know that. So, we gotta do what we have to until something changes. That ain't my fault."

She popped her head back and scrunched her face. "Oh, so it's mine? And what are you talking about kicking it? I'm not trying to kick it with you,

Jayden. I'm trying to get you to man up, and step away from the streets so we can raise this child together that is growing inside of me." She pushed me away. "Go back over there. I can't be beside you right now. I'm not on that. It's only going to make me more emotionally dependent on you, and right now, that isn't what's best. I just can't be. It's literally killing me." She blinked, and more tears slid down her cheeks.

I pulled her to me while she continued to fight me away. "Baby, please stop now, come on. We can figure this thing out. I'm not trying to hurt you, and I ain't going nowhere. I'm trying my best to be smart about everything and keep both of our best interests at heart, but I see I'm messing up, so teach me. Tell me what I'm supposed to do, 'cause I'm a street nigga and I can't let this shit go with Nico. I just can't."

She pushed me away. "Go on the other side, Jayden. I'm serious."

I got up and walked around to the other side of the booth, feeling both angry and a little hurt. I couldn't believe that she was acting the way that she was. I felt like we were on the verge of ending, and I couldn't have that. I loved her too much.

She ran her fingers through her curly hair as the waitress came over and set our plates and drinks in front of us, before smiling and walking off.

Whitney moved her plate to the side and looked across the table at me. "Is Myeesha really your blood cousin, or are you guys just play cousins like most people are in Philly?" She grabbed her glass of juice and sipped out of it.

"That's my real cousin. Why you ask me that?" I picked up a steak fry and put it into my mouth.

She shrugged. "I just wanted to know. The first night that she was in Philly, and you were just getting home, after spending some time with your mother I thought that I would come downstairs and cuddle up with my man and give you some of my body, but when I got to your bedroom door it was locked. Me being me, I'm nosy; but so what; I placed my ear to your door and heard a bunch of moaning and the squeaking of your bed. So, naturally, I knew you was in there fucking somebody, and I just didn't think it was her, because you know, she was supposed to be your cousin and all. I guess that don't mean nothing. Silly me, huh?" She shook her head.

I lowered my own head, and for a second, I couldn't even make eye contact with her. I knew I was bogus, and what's crazy is that while me and Myeesha were doing our thing, it excited me more because I knew we could have been caught by her or my mother. For me that made playing in her pussy all the better. I was sick, and I knew it.

Whitney smiled weakly. "I wasn't trying to make you feel some type of way, Jayden. I mean, you and I never said that we couldn't screw other people, so I don't feel like you cheated on me or nothing. I was just surprised that you had the nerve to fuck your cousin while me and your mother was right upstairs." She laughed sarcastically, then picked up her cheeseburger and took a bite out of it.

"We ain't fuck that night, for the record, so stop saying that."

She laughed with a mouth full of food. "Not that night, huh? Well, y'all most definitely did by now." She said, moving the food into her right jaw so she could talk, and I still could barely make the words out. "You good though. Just keep doing you." She smiled, and I could still see the tear-streaks along her cheeks.

I reached into my pocket and pulled out the $5,000 that I'd brought to give to her, just to make sure that she was straight. I reached across the table, picked up her Gucci purse and put it inside of it. "I'm sorry if I hurt you, but I need you to know that I love you, and that I will always be here for you. I just gotta handle my business before I can sit down and be a family man. When it's all said and done, I will be that one that you can depend on for everything. I promise you that. It won't be long."

She picked up her purse and flicked her thumb over the money that I'd placed inside of it. "This guilt money, huh? Well, let me show you how I feel about this guilt money." She took it all out of her purse, placed a gee to the side, then ripped the money to shreds, before throwing it in my face and getting up. "I don't want yo' fucking money, Jayden. I want you to be a man, not a thug. Our child deserves that. When you get yourself together, hit me up. Until then, I'm cutting you off just like I did Nico. Screw the both of y'all." She left the table, walked over to the waitress, tapped her on the shoulder, then handed her the thousand dollars in cash before looking back at me with anger in her eyes. Afterward, she opened the door and left the restaurant, just as Jackson and Peretti's bitch ass was coming into it.

I felt like I was going to throw up as they slid in the booth in front of me.

Jackson picked up one of the steak fries from Whitney's plate and put it into his mouth, chewing with his mouth open. "What's the matter? Trouble in paradise?"

"Yeah, you starting to feel like you killed Lincoln for a woman that wasn't worth it?" Peretti added. He laughed for a second before his face turned into a frown. "What type of dealings did you have with Pablo, the boss of the Mexican Posse? Word on the street is that one of your underlings popped him at the BP gas station over on Morgan Street. Care to shed some light on the situation for us?"

I curled my upper lip and looked from one to the other. I had visions of killing them both, right where they sat. I hated these pigs more than Muslims hated pork. They disgusted me. On top of that, my heart was hurting over what had just went down between me and Whitney. I wanted to get up and chase her down, beg her to not go, to love me like I did her despite my weaknesses. I knew there was no better woman on this earth for me than her.

Jackson picked up the pieces of torn money and looked across the table at me with a huge smile on his face. "I suppose she wouldn't take your blood money?"

"Look, I don't know shit about no fucking Mexicans, and I didn't kill Lincoln. Why the fuck are you Swine following me?" I asked, sliding my hand down to the handle of my gun.

Peretti held up a hand. "Whoa, now, Chief. We're just following up on intel from a very reliable CI, and in the process trying to stop a bloody war from brewing on our streets. The Mexican Posse aren't the ones to be fucked with. They have an arm that stretches all the way into the heart of Mexico. You have no idea what type of mafia that you're screwing around with."

I looked into his eyes with hatred and lowered mine. "Like I said, I don't know shit about no Mexicans, and I didn't kill Lincoln. Whoever your CI is can kiss my black ass." I stood up and looked down on them while Jackson popped another steak fry into his mouth. "For the record, I'm only gon' let you muhfuckas come at me so many times before it really starts to bother me. Trust me on this."

Jackson sucked his fingers one at a time. "Well, lucky for us you won't be on the streets that much longer."

Chapter 7

I felt the sweat pouring down my back and my boxers ticking to me, as I watched the Puerto Rican reach inside of the brown Ford Aerostar and take out four large chests, setting them on the concrete inside of the old recycling warehouse that was located on Hadley Drive.

He kneeled, took the screwdriver that was in his hand and popped one of them open. "Check this out, Papi. This is what you came for, am I right?" He asked, waving me over.

Behind him were three other Rican men with black wife beaters on and who had semi-automatic weapons in their hands.

I walked over to him with two Forty-Fives in my waistband. I kneeled to check out the weaponry, picking one of the M-4's up, and turned it over in my hand. "Yeah, this boy nice right here." I popped the clip out and checked to see if it was loaded. It blew my mind when I discovered that it in fact was.

"That's some serious fire power right there, PaPa. You squeeze that trigger and it lets off thirty rounds in less than three seconds, lighting a nigga's ass on fire. I brought twenty with me. I want five a piece; that's the new deal." He stood up and looked over my shoulder at Kilroy who had a fully automatic Uzi in his hand and a mug on his face.

I'd watched him get high as a kite before this meeting, and I was a little worried that he was off of his square. I was thankful that Poppa had come with us. He appeared to be more level headed and on point. Like me, he didn't do dope before he bussed moves. He felt like he would miss something or make a mistake, and we both knew there was no room for that.

"Say, Kilroy, you good, baby? You're giving me this weird look that I never seen in your eyes before." The Rican said, lowering his eyes.

Kilroy nodded. "Just making sure yo' niggas don't do nothing stupid while my boss is right there." He scrunched his face and lowered his eyes.

The Rican shook his head. "N'all, PaPa, it's all good. We're all friends here. Am I right?"

Poppa walked over with the two briefcases full of money and placed them at my feet before backing away with his Mach 11 in his hand. Like Kilroy, he never took his eyes off of the Rican's men.

I pointed to the suitcases with the M-4. "There's your money. We'll take them all. Count it to confirm that it's all there."

The Rican kneeled and popped open one of the cases, immediately revealing the cash inside of it. He picked up one of the stacks and flicked through it with a big smile on his face. Then, he put one down and flicked through another one, nodding. "Okay, I've seen all that I needed to. We're good to go." He turned around and signaled to one of his men.

As soon as he did that, the man lowered his weapon and bent over to pick up the first suitcase of weapons.

The Rican leaned down to pick up the second briefcase with a big smile on his face. "You my nigga, Kilroy. You're a great business ma—"

Boom-boom-boom!

I'd slipped the M-4 off of safety before angling the barrel so that it was at the back of his head. The bullet slammed into the back of his skull and knocked his brains out the front of his face before he fell forward, shaking on the pavement. I ducked and turned toward his men, letting my M-4 ride in their direction while Kilroy and Poppa chopped them down.

Their bodies flew up against the side of their van, vibrating in the air while our bullets ripped into their flesh, filling them with hole after hole. The warehouse was cloudy with gun smoke, and the scent of gun powder was heavy in the air along with blood and hot metal.

I felt the sweat sliding down the side of my face and along the collar of my neck.

* * *

I gave Kilroy a half of hug, then did the same to Poppa as we held the M-4's in our hands. I had a bottle of Ace of Spades that I'd popped the cork on. I felt like celebrating since everything had gone well. "Now, that's how you handle business, my niggas. We got in, and we got out."

"Yeah, and now we ready to go to war with Trump bitch ass if we need to. Armed and muthafucking dangerous!" Kilroy hollered in the hot basement in one of the buildings out in DC.

"Yo, I say we ride down on them Mexicans tonight. Let's chop they ass down and come on back out here and get some sleep. I know they ain't gon' be expecting us to come at them this fast, so it'll be smart. Nah'mean?" I said, remembering the shit that

Jackson and Peretti had said about the Mexicans being all powerful and shit. That irritated me to my very core.

Poppa nodded. "Whatever we do, let's get it over with and get back to getting money. Tomorrow the first, and the feens gon' be all through this bitch, ready to go broke. I'm trying to have a half a million before 2019 come in." He popped the clip out of his M-4 and set it on the table. Then, he looked through the scope, smiling.

Naz came into the basement and hung up his phone. "Yo, I got one for you, Jayden. That nigga Nico gon' be at Robert's pool hall tonight. He supposed to be having a meeting with them niggas from the Bronx. Robert contacted me personally to let me know and asked me what I wanna do. So, what are you thinking?"

Kilroy stood up and laughed. "I say we hit both of they ass. Why not? Half of us can go and chop down the Mexican Posse, and the other can go and see if we can catch that nigga Nico slipping coming out of Robert's. I'd take either or. I just wanna kill something else tonight. Word is bond." He picked his M-4 up off the table and cocked it.

I frowned as I imagined my bullets ripping into Nico's face like they had the back of the Rican's head. I would love to see his brains on the outside of his body where they belonged. "Yo, as much as I wanna fuck over them Mexicans, I wanna body that fool Nico ten times more. I'm tired of him breathing and fucking with the law every chance that he get. The longer this nigga is alive, the more enemies we take on. That's including the law and the streets. This punk coming from all angles."

"Yeah, but he comin' like a bitch though. He ain't bringing that iron like we tryin' to. He went all the way out to New York to bring over some niggas that's supposed to be about that life, and them niggas ain't did shit yet. I say we go over and try and kill all they ass. Word is fucking bond." Naz said, slurring his words a little bit.

I nodded. "What we gotta realize is that if we heat up the streets of Philly like this all in one night, then Alphabet Boys gon' be all over our asses if they catch wind. And it's CI's everywhere. So, we gotta be prepared to cover our tracks and be as careful as possible. If we even think that a muhfucka is a rat, it's in our best interest to cut they fucking head off and rip their tongues out of their throats. If a killa like Nico can turn into Twelve, then nobody can be trusted. That's a fact." I sat on the couch and rubbed my temples, already trying to envision how the night would go.

"Aiight then, me and Jayden will holler at Nico 'nem, and you and Poppa can fuck over the Mexicans. I say we take a few hours to get our heads together and meet back here at three." Kilroy said, dumping cocaine out on to the table, chopping through it with a razor blade.

I looked at my phone and saw that it was ten at night. That would give us five hours to get situated. It was time that I needed to clear my head because I couldn't shake Whitney out of my mind. I wondered if in that very moment she was thinking about me, so I sent her over a text, only to find out that she'd blocked my number. That was a blow to my heart. I had to get from down there with my niggas because I felt like I was on the verge of having an emotional break down, though at the time I didn't know what that looked or felt like. My heart hurt, and I didn't like the feel of it. I was willing to do anything to make that pain go away because I had never felt it before.

* * *

I pulled the chair away from the night table that was on the side of the hotel room's bed. Myeesha was walking past me, on her way to grab a slice of pizza from the Pizza Hut box, with her black lace panties all in her ass. I pulled her over to me, and she straddled me immediately, looking into my eyes while I grabbed a hold of that ass.

"What's the matter with you, Jayden? You seem real down and have been ever since you got here tonight." She rubbed my eyebrows, smiled, and kissed my lips softly. "Hmm?"

I rubbed all over her ass and squeezed the cheeks in my hands. "It's nothing. It's just my heart is hurting, that's all. It's a new experience for me. I don't like this shit." I lowered my head and shook it, trying to get a hold of myself.

I was wondering what Whitney was doing in that moment. Was she thinking about me, or was she fucking with some random nigga to try and get me off of her mind like I was trying to do her? I wished that I had said the right words to her. I wished that I could change on a dime and be all of the man that she needed me to be, but I couldn't. The streets were embedded too deep within my soul. I didn't know if I could ever be a one woman type of nigga. I found the female body way too alluring, and the more forbidden the situation, the more it excited me and made me want to go

hard while trying it out. Especially if the forbidden prospect was as bad as Myeesha.

She frowned and grabbed my face into her manicured hands. "I hope you talking about the love you got for me and not some other bitch, because I'm right in your face and I ain't thinking about nobody else but you, and yo' fine ass." She rubbed me face and looked into my eyes. "But it's not me that got your heart feeling that way, is it?"

I took a deep breath and looked into her green eyes, tryingnot to get mesmerized by her beauty, but it was so hard. I didn't care if she was my cousin or not, had I seen her anywhere in the streets— it could have been on my wedding day— I would've had to have her. She was that damn bad to me, and her pussy was fire. I shook my head and refused to look into her eyes any longer. I felt myself getting aroused, and the picture of Whitney in my head was fading fast. That forbidden pussy was a problem for me, I ain't gon' even lie.

"Is it your baby mother, or that girl that say she pregnant with your child?" She asked, lifting my chin so she could look into my eyes, while she softly rubbed the side of my face.

I nodded. "Yeah, I saw her today, and things didn't go so well. She feeling like I ain't been holding her down in the way I'm supposed to, ever since she been pregnant. Kind of called me immature and all type of shit. Even ripped up four thousand dollars in cash and gave another gee away to some random waitress, even though I wasn't knocking that part, 'cause at least she ain't rip it up like the rest of it." I exhaled loudly. "I don't know what to do."

She picked my head up and kissed my lips, still rubbing the side of my face soothingly. "Jayden, you are way too fine to be sitting here tripping over some broad, especially when you don't need nobody but me. I'm right here and I'll be everything that you need. I've already decided to chill for a while and say fuck Atlanta. You see, it didn't take me that long to become addicted to your ass all over again. That girl just don't know what she got. She's expecting too much. Y'all are too young for that shit. What type of female rips up four thousand dollars? It's hard out here, fa real." She laid her cheek against mine and rubbed it back and forth before kissing my ear. "Is there anything that I can do for you to take your mind off of her?" She licked my earlobe, then sucked on it.

I squeezed her ass, pulled her firmly to my chest, before kissing her lips and sliding my tongue into her mouth. "Make me forget about her, cuz. Tell me that everything gon' be alright, and that I ain't crapping on her or nothing. I'm more of a man than that." I said, trying to get Whitney's crying eyes out of my mind. I was missing her so bad.

Myeesha humped forward and trapped my torso with in her thick thighs. Her hot pussy radiated through the crotch of her lace panties, searing my stomach. The scent of her perfume caused my dick to rise to its full length. Its head poked out of my waistband, throbbing like crazy.

"I love you Jayden, and I'll be everything that you need. I've been by your side ever since we were real little kids, and I've always been crazy about you. You got you a bad bitch right here. You got you a rider right here. I'll be everything that she was to you and more, I promise." She wrapped her arms around my neck, while I held her tighter and rubbed her back, noting the fact that she didn't have a bra on under her tight, pink and black beater.

"I love you too Myeesha, and that's the shit I need to hear, baby. I need to hear that you got me, no matter what." Even though I said this, I couldn't get Whitney out of my mind. I felt like she was some sort of drug that I was addicted to, and I couldn't kick the habit no matter how hard I tried.

Myeesha rubbed all over my naked chest, biting into her bottom lip. "I am your rider and I would never leave you under no circumstances. You belong to me and I belong to you. Ain't shit finna come between us." She said, sliding out of my lap and onto her knees, pulling my boxers down.

My dick sprang up like a brown cucumber. She wrapped her small hand around it and pumped it, sniffing the head, before sucking just the head of it into her mouth and taking her hands away.

"Make me see you and not her, Myeesha. State yo' claim, baby, right now. That's all you gotta do."

I spread my legs and watched her swallow my whole pipe, gag, and bring her mouth all the way up to the tip before sucking it again. I grabbed a handful of her hair to guide her while she sucked my dick, looking into my eyes.

Visions of the time I'd spent with Whitney continuously invaded my thoughts. I saw Whitney's pretty face and heard her laughing inside of my mind. I saw us feeding each other and then imagined her face full of tears. The sight of it made me want to break down. I couldn't take that emotional shit. It was killing me. I stood up, still grabbing Myeesha by the hair, and slung her across the bed violently.

"Uhhh!" she screamed, looking back at me.

I pulled her panties all the way down her legs and placed my forearm into her back while I kicked her legs apart. Then, I rubbed my dick up and down her wet pussy before slamming it home with brute force.

"Uhhh! Fuck, yes!" She screamed, looking back at me then closing her eyes. "Fuck me, cuz. It's okay. Take yo' frustrations out on this pussy. It's good."

I pulled her to me by her small waist and plunged my dick deep into her stomach from the back, before fucking her with anger. I needed to cum. I had to release my seed within her. I knew if I could then I could get Whitney off of my brain. I just needed Myeesha's pussy to conquer me, so I watched my dick shoot in and out of her while she held her cheeks apart.

"Un, un, un, un, un, un, un, Jayden, slow down! Un, un, please, slow. Down. You killing me. You. Fucking. Me. Too. Hard. Uhhhh, shit, yes!" She screamed, slamming back into me, trying to keep up pace with my pistoling pipe, though I was making it hard to do so.

I reached under her and took a hold of her swinging titties. "Pull that beater up. Let me feel these titties, Myeesha. Hurry up. I wanna feel all over you like I used to when everybody was sleep in the house. You remember that shit? Huh?" I asked, stabbing into her faster and faster.

"Yes! Yes! " She hollered, pulling her beater all the way up so her titties were free. Her hard nipples were scraping against the bed sheets before I started to pull on them. "Fuck yes!"

I felt all over her body while I worked that forbidden pussy. It was wet and making loud, slushy noises that drove me crazy. I felt myself getting ready to cum deep within her womb.

She humped back real hard and broke our connection, climbing on the bed and laying her head on the blankets with her ass in the air. She had both of her cheeks spread wide. "Fuck me in here, Jayden. I want you to take your anger out on this big booty. Please. It's yours, cuz. Come on!" She reached under herself, rubbing her clit furiously; pinching it, then rubbing the juices in the crinkle of her asshole.

I jumped on the bed and got behind her. Leaning forward, I sucked her ring, then sliding my tongue inside of her backdoor, slobbering allover, it on purpose while she fingered herself at full speed.

"Unnn, you want that ass, don't you, cuz? You been wanting to fuck me in my ass, ain't you?" She purred, then spread her cheeks for me again.

I got behind her and eased my dick into her backdoor, while she groaned in pleasure and pain. I was biting into my bottom lip as I watched the head penetrate her, feeling that taboo asshole surround my manhood. "Hell yeah, you already know that. Remember we tried when I was thirteen, but it hurt too bad?"

She slammed backward and sucked my whole dick into her backdoor. "Not no more. I'm ready now. Fuck yo' baby momma. Fuck me. I need you, cuz." She licked her thick lips and closed her eyes tighter.

I slammed forward, pulled back and slammed forward again until I picked up a savage rhythm and got to fucking her ass like a porn star. *Bam, bam, bam, bam.*

"Un, uh, uh, yes, yes, yes, fuck my ass! Fuck. My. Ass. Fuck it. Fuck it harder! Uhh, I love it!"

I was going crazy by this point, diving in and out of that ass while she went and did her thing to her pussy below. I watched her titties jiggle like crazy and I wondered what her father would say if he knew how I had her lil' ass bent up, fucking her ass from the back like I was mad at her, and loving every second of it because it felt so good, and it was so wrong at the same time.

She slammed back into my lap. "I'm finna cum Jayden. Uh, shit, I'm finna cum. Keep fucking my ass. It's yours, lil' cuz. It's yours!" She spread her pussy lips and pulled on her clit, flicking it with her middle finger from side to side, before shaking into my lap like she was having a seizure. "Ahhhh! Fuck!" She fell on her stomach with me still pounding at her guts.

I flipped her on her side and kept on digging deeper and deep, watching watching my dick go in and out of her golden ass, until I couldn't take it no more. "This my shit, Myeesha. This ass belongs to me, you hear me! Do you hear meeeeee!" I hollered, jerking and cumming deep within her bowels while she squeezed her asshole around my dick, over and over, milking me.

"Unn, yes, I hear you, baby. It's yours. Ooo-a, I feel your cum. It's yours, baby. Mmmm."

Ghost

Chapter 8

Kilroy parked the stolen whip a block away, and I looked up the street towards Robert's Pool Hall, cocking the M-4 in my hand, and lowering my mask. I could see that there were four trucks parked in front of the small pool hall, just as Robert told us there would be.

"Yo, I'm letting you know right now, Jayden, I'm killing every muhfucka up in there, just like we should. Like you said, we don't know who's a snitch and who ain't, so we gotta knock niggas' heads off with no remorse. That includes Robert's head as well. Fuck him. It is what it is. Nah'mean?" Kilroy cocked his M-4 and pulled down his mask, looking down the street toward Robert's pool hall and scanning the area just like I was.

"Yo, that's exactly how I need you to think. From here on out, we gotta be rotten to the core; fucking niggas over to send a message that our crew ain't to be played with. So, let's handle business." I took my seatbelt from around me and looked in the backseat at the three soldiers that Kilroy had brought along with him. They were members of the Shooters, neither one older than the age of sixteen, but all proven to have had cold hearts, passing tests that Kilroy, Naz and Poppa had put them through time and time again. "Y'all ready back there?"

They nodded in unison and pulled their masks over their faces before cocking the M-4s that they held.

"Yo, I'ma pull around to the back alley, that way he can enter through the backdoor that Robert left open for us. Them niggas should be upfront where we usually play pool at. Robert said they pushed some tables together so they could have their little meeting. I say we run in that bitch and chop everything, empty all of these clips. Fuck it." Kilroy said, pulling away from the curb. He rolled past the pool hall and I saw that the blinds were pulled down, making it impossible for us to see inside of it.

"Yo, what's the deal with Robert anyway? Why he selling Nico and his crew out? You must've made some type of deal with him."

Kilroy nodded. "That fool Robert ain't nothing but a dope head now. He ain't the smooth-talking player that we knew back in the day. Now that fool got a habit. He want us to kill these niggas and then burn the place down so he can collect the insurance. I hear the Irish mafia all up his ass because he owe them a lot of money from gambling." He shrugged. "I don't know, but he's dead anyway. Fuck him." He pulled into the alley a few buildings down from Robert's Pool Hall and threw the car in park, looking over his shoulder at the crew of young killas that he'd brought with us for the job. "Look, I don't want y'all going in there playing no muthafucking games. The objective is to leave that bitch in a blood bath. Take these niggas' heads off and get the fuck back out. Aiight?" He looked from on to the other.

They nodded in unison and began to file out of the car, waiting in the alley until we got out.

I allowed for Kilroy to lead the way since it was my first time ever going to Robert's Pool Hall and he was familiar with the area and the path we needed to take to get to the backdoor of the hall.

The alley was dark and without any lights, other than that what came from the moon in the sky. I ducked as best as I could and tried to keep pace with Kilroy. Even though he was a bit heavy-set, he moved real light on his feet, and I was having a hard time lugging around the big M-4 being hunched over at the same time.

There were dogs barking off in the distance and the sound of a male and a female arguing on the next block. I could also hear the traffic from the busy street that the pool hall was located on. My ribs began to bother me the longer I was bent over, until finally we made it to back of the pool hall where there was a five-foot metal gate that we had to jumped over. First Kilroy, then me, and then the rest of our lil' crew. Once we were in the back of the place, Kilroy crept up to the big, brown door and tried the handle. I watched it open just a crack.

He looked over his shoulder at me. "Aiight, so far so good. Remember, they gon' be in the front. When we first go in through this door, we gon' be in the kitchen. When we leave the kitchen, we turn right, and then go all the way to the front. We should be able to hit them bitches from a distance. Hopefully, Nico bitch ass is sitting at the table 'cause Robert said he is here so we'll see. Let's do this, bruh." He lowered his eyes, nodded, then turned back and slowly opened the door. After he peeked inside, he ran in.

A second later I was on his heels, crouching with my M-4 against my shoulder, ready to fire and knock a nigga's head off. It was just like Kilroy had said, when we first got inside we were in a big kitchen that looked filthy.

It looked like it had not been tended to in at least three days. There were dishes and pots and pans in the sink. The floor was caked with muddy footprints. There was a mop bucket full of dirty water in the middle of the floor, and it smelled like spoiled milk all around. I didn't give a fuck how hungry I could have been if I was just coming to that pool hall to chill, I would have never eaten shit from there. Aside from the smells, the dirty dishes and all of that, there were big ass cock roaches everywhere I looked. I couldn't believe my eyes.

Kilroy acted as if none of that bothered him. He stopped right at the door of the kitchen, crouched and peeked around the corner, looking for a long time it felt. Then, he nodded at me and waved for us to follow him before he hit it down the hallway with me on his heels.

My heart was beating faster and faster. From my vantage point I could see that there was in fact a table full of niggas with blue rags around their necks and had long ass dreads. They were passing around a bottle of VSOP, talking loudly, and it appeared that they were also playing cards, but I couldn't quite see that until me and Kilroy bum rushed them. There was no talking at first, just shooting.

Bocka, bocka, bocka, bocka! The M-4 jumped in my hands with a big burst of fire spitting out of its barrel. I watched two of my bullets slam into the face of a heavy-set, yellow-skinned dude. He had just put the bottle of VSOP to his lips before my bullets slammed into his forehead and knocked the top of it off his face. He flew backward and landed on his side with blood gushing out of him.

Kilroy rushed the table, chopping the men down with no remorse. His bullets ripping into their flesh, sending them running in every direction, but there was no escape. If his bullets did not hit them, then mine did, or the ones from our young shooters who were emptying their clips and reloading. They were about twelve deep, and Nico was nowhere in sight.

After we chopped them down, the air was full of gun smoke, and the floors were full of blood and plasma. I watched a few of the men shaking on the pavement, struggling for their lasts breaths before Kilroy stood over them and finished them off with a heart of ice.

"Robert! Robert! Where the fuck you at, man? Bring yo' ass out here right now!" He hollered, turning around and going down the hallway that we'd just come from.

I followed him, paranoid as fuck. We had made a lot of noise and my biggest worry was that someone had heard it and had contacted the police. I wanted to get up out of there, plus the smell of burnt flesh was getting the better of me. I waved for our young shooters to follow. "Come on, y'all, let's get up out of here."

Before we got halfway down the hallway, the manager's door opened, and Robert stuck his yellow, freckled face out of it. "Kilroy, is that you, young blood?" He asked with his eyes bucked.

Kilroy ran up and grabbed him by the neck. "Bitch ass nigga! Where is Nico? You said he'd be here!" He hollered through clenched teeth.

Robert gagged as sweat slid down the side of his face. "He was, man. He left right before you came. Said he had some other business to tend to and that he would be back in a lil' while. That was right before you came, I swear." He whimpered, looking Kilroy in the eyes. "You know I wouldn't lie to you, man."

Kilroy shook his head. "Nigga, I don't know shit." He pushed him back, aimed his M-4 and popped him three quick times in the face. *Boom, boom, boom.*

Robert dropped to the floor with his face slamming into the carpet, hard. A puddle of blood formed around him almost immediately.

"Fuck nigga. Let's get out of here, y'all. We'll find Nico's bitch ass at another time." He said, before taking off down the hall.

We ran full speed until we were out of the pool hall, just as sirens sounded somewhere close by. The only thing going through my head is that we'd just killed a bunch of niggas and neither one of them was Nico. I was pissed and growing more and more frustrated by the minute.

* * *

After getting out of the hotel's shower, I wrapped the huge, white, fluffy robe around my body, grabbed the remote and turned on the television so I could watch the news. I turned to the channel that broadcasted out of Philly, just as Myeesha slid on the bed beside me and laid her head on my shoulder.

"I can tell that you're tense, Jayden. You must've had to handle some business tonight, huh?" She asked, rubbing the back of my head and then kissing my covered shoulder.

I had turned the caption on so I could read what the reporters were saying at the bottom of the screen. So far, they were reporting that there had been a massive shooting at a local pool hall. That many had been fatally injured, but they were unable to release any details at the moment. Then, in other news, there had been another mass shooting on the city's east side where many people were found dead. This was also under investigation and they would keep the public updated whenever they found out any new information. I flipped the television off and curled my upper lip. Nico's bitch ass was heavy on my mind. I wanted him six feet deep, buried and sleeping with worms. The fact that he was still alive made my flesh crawl.

I looked down at Myeesha and nodded. "Yeah, I had to take care of some minor things. You can tell that something ain't right, huh?" I asked, as she rubbed the side of my face.

She straddled my lap, causing her short, silk robe to rise above her waist. She looked into my eyes with her pure green ones, holding the sides of my face. "Jayden, you already know that I know how you get down. You've always been about that life, and I've always been drawn to that part of you." She kissed my lips and rubbed our noses together with her eyes closed. She smelled like Prada.

I wrapped my arms around her small waist and held her on top of me. She felt so good and so hot. There was something about her lil' ass that had me feeling some type of way. I couldn't help it. I kissed her on the neck, sniffing her up and loving the scent of her natural body mixed with the perfume.

She sat straight up and placed her hands on my shoulders, looking into my eyes. "You ever thought about running away from here? Maybe starting a new life somewhere else?" She took a deep breath and slowly blew it out.

I shook my head. "N'all, I haven't. Philly is where my heart is. It's my slums and it's all I know. I wouldn't even know what to do outside of here. Everybody ain't plugged like Meek Mill, nah'mean?" I smiled weakly, then saw a vision of Nico in my head, causing me to shake it.

Myeesha held my chin and looked into my eyes again. "I'm serious, Jayden. I'm worried about you. You don't think I know about all of this shit that you're into? I know you're beefing with Nico, and I know he went to the Bronx and got a bunch of niggas to come down here and kill you. I also know that that's probably them niggas on the news." She laughed for a second and then her face was serious again. "What if I told you I could put you up on a move that would leave us straight for a long, long time? That there was a reason I came up here to see you in the first place, and that I haven't been completely honest with you? Would you be mad at me, or would you be happy in the fact that I got something to bring to the table?" She asked, running her thumb over my lips before sucking it into her mouth.

I stood up, picking her up at the same time, and tossed her on the bed so fast that she yelped while in the air. "Fuck, Myeesha! Don't you know that I'm dealing with all kinds of betrayals and muhfuckas lying to my face already? The last person I need to be doing that shit is you. You're supposed to be my backbone right now. Don't you understand that shit?" I asked, looking at her with my anger building. My heart pounded in my chest. I needed to calm down. I hated when I got how I was, but I could not control it.

Myeesha lowered her head then looked up at me with those sexy ass green eyes, blinking them a few times to lay on her girly charm. Even though it turned me on, it pissed me off even more because I was serious. I didn't like her lying to me about nothing. We were supposed to have been better than that. For as long as I had known her, I had never lied to her one time.

"But, baby, I didn't mean to keep it from you or reveal what my true intentions were. I guess I was just looking for the right time, and when one thing started to pop up right after the other, I figured I'd better let you know what was good or we'd miss the window of opportunity."

I ran my hands over my face and exhaled, blowing air through my nostrils, shaking my head slowly. "Aiight, tell me what's good. How much paper you talking? And this shit better be good too?" I walked over to the bed and stood over her.

She crawled across it until she came to the edge where I could reach her, looking up at me the whole time. "But first, can you just say that you forgive me, because I can't have you mad at me and stuff. I can't take that right now. I love you too much." She took a finger and started to bite on the nail, sitting back on her haunches with her knees spread.

The gown had moved around her waist so I could see her naked pussy lips. They were fat and engorged. Her inner lips poked out just below her outer ones. I thought she looked so fucking sexy that I was seconds away from taking that pussy on some savage shit.

I grabbed a handful of her hair and yanked her head toward me, leaning into her face. "From here on out, you bet not ever lie to me again or lead me astray. You better be more than one hunnit 'cause I ain't gon' play with yo' ass. You here me, ma?" I asked her though clenched teeth.

She nodded. "Yes, baby. I hear you, and I'm sorry. I promise I won't do nothing like that ever again." She whimpered with her eyes closed.

I noted that her robe had opened a little more. Now both of her pretty titties were exposed. Her brown nipples were on full display. Both were hard and standing tall from their mounds. I pushed her head backward, letting go of her hair. She yelped again and fell back on the bed.

"Now tell me what's good?" I said, sitting down on the bed.

She climbed out of it, came to kneel between my legs, opening my robe to take my pipe inside her small hands. "Ooh, I love how you be treating me. You don't care how fine I am. You still stand on my neck, and that shit makes my pussy so wet. I wish you could beat my kitty in right now. Just hurt me like only you can, Jayden." She sucked my head into her mouth and bobbed up and down on it for thirty seconds before popping it out of her mouth. "I got this nigga that own like four strip clubs down in Atlanta. I mean, he sells heroin and all types of pills too, but his strip clubs are his cover. It's a long story, so I'll just tell you the gist. He's in love with me, and he's asked me to marry him, giving me the option of giving him my answer after I get back from visiting you guys up here because I told him that I couldn't make a decision while my brain was clogged up with the things that were taking place with you." She sucked my dick back into her mouth, then deep-throated it ten long times before popping it back out and rubbing it along her cheek.

"Anyway, he has two million dollars in cash put up inside of the home that we share together. I want you to come down and hit his ass. Rob him blind, and even kill him if you have to. I don't care because I don't feel anything for him. Never have. I met him in a club and I saw an opportunity to come up. That's it, that's all. Plus, it's not like he ain't fucking with a bunch of bitches no way. He's a player and I think the only reason he wants to marry me is because of my exotic looks. Just a typical man if you asked me. But all I care about is you, Jayden. You run this shit. I'll fuck over any nigga or any bitch for you. That's on my mother." She kissed my dick head again, rubbing it along her neck with her eyes closed. "If we can get this two million plus dollars from him, would you leave the streets alone and run away with me to somewhere else besides Philly? Please, baby?" She begged, gazing into my eyes.

I put my fingers into her hair and pulled on it a little bit, enough to cause her a little pain, but not so much that it hurt her too bad. I already knew how to handle a dime real rough in order for them to get the message. Myeesha was so bad that whenever a nigga saw her, the first thing they would do is fawn all over her and treat her like a queen because they thought it was how you got her, but it wasn't. She was used to that treatment; had gotten it her whole life, so she steadily looked for a man that would stand on her fine ass.

A man that wouldn't necessarily treat her like shit, but he'd let her know that it wasn't sweet, and that she wasn't all that, even though she kind of was. Mental manipulation was a muhfucka.

I nodded at her, stood up and pulled her to her feet, while I kept a handful of her hair. I brought my fingers down until I was groping her long, bronzed neck. "So, you saying you know for a fact that this nigga got that amount of bread put up? There ain't one doubt in your mind?" I tilted her chin upward so she could look into my eyes like she had a habit of doing anyway.

She sucked on her bottom lip and took a hold of my pipe in her hand, squeezing it. "I know that one hundred percent, but what I want to do is to fly back to Atlanta in a few days and scope everything out just to make sure because he is very loose around me. When I know for sure that everything is as it was before I left, I'll send for you. You'll come down and handle your business, then we can move on with our lives. I just never want to be without you ever again, so let me do my part to make that official. Oh, and we might have to take my little sister, Miah, with us, wherever we go. I just want to save her before the streets overtake her like they did us. She has a bright future ahead of her. I just gotta get her away from Atlanta. Is that cool?" She asked, stroking my pipe, pressing the head against her hot stomach. She was smearing my pre-cum all over her golden skin, 'causing my pipe to become harder.

I nodded, leaning forward to suck her juicy lips into my mouth. "Yeah, it's good. Long as we can get our hands on that type of bread, then all should be well. You gotta get down there as soon as possible so you can make sure that everything is everything, and we'll go from there." I picked her up, making her wrap her thick thighs around me before we fell to the bed.

Ghost

Chapter 9

Two days later, and with the humidity in Philly worse than I could ever remember it being, me and Myeesha stood in the direct sunlight with our tongues wrestling and me feeling all over that Gucci covered ass while she moaned into my mouth, with her first-class plane ticket in her hand. I didn't even want her to leave. I felt like I could hit that pussy every single day, all day long, and never get tired of it. It seemed like the more we fucked, the freakier she became until nothing was off limits. I'd gotten used to fucking that ass at least once a day, now she would be back in Georgia and I'd be feening for her until we were united again.

I cuffed them cheeks and licked all over her neck before sucking on her lips again, while she humped into me with a bunch of people looking at us like we were crazy. I didn't care. She had me sexually and physically dependent on her ass. Emotionally I was still all about Whitney, but Myeesha did have me feeling some type of way.

I broke our embrace and held her small waist, looking into them green eyes. "Now, listen to me. You already know what I got going on up here. I'm in a crazy war that I gotta handle before I move anywhere else. That nigga Nico gotta pay for his sins. That's just that. So even if you hear about some bullshit going on up here, you stick to the plan, because I will be down there to handle business in a week from today, no matter what. When I get down, we'll fuck this nigga over, take that cash, snatch up Miah, and bounce. I don't know to where yet, but we'll figure that out at a later date. Do you hear me?" I asked, watching her long hair blow in the dry wind.

She smiled and nodded. "Yes, I hear you, and I got you. I just really need for you to be careful because I need you so freaking bad. Just looking at you right now is making it hard for me to leave you, Jayden. I feel like a little girl all over again. Like the summer is ending and we have to split up because school is starting back. I hate this." She stomped her left red and pink Jordan that matched her Gucci fit and urse. Her thick thigh jiggled before she stepped forward and wrapped her arms around my neck. "I love you, baby. Please don't forget about me, or the fact of how much I need you and only you. I'm so serious."

I rubbed all over that ass, sniffing her up my nostrils with my eyes closed. I was trying to relish the moment because the fact of the matter was that I didn't know if I would ever see her again. I knew that I was living on borrowed time. That if Nico or his crew didn't get me, then there was the Mexican Posse, any of my old enemies, or even Twelve. I knew they were lurking around, and it was only a matter of time before they came for me. There was a big target on my back from all angles, but it was all a part of being in the slums of Philly. It was all I knew, and I lived for that sadistic shit.

I kissed Myeesha's lips one more time. "I got you, boo. You know I'm hard to kill. I'll be there in one week. That's my word."

She looked into my eyes for a long time, sucking on her bottom lip before nodding and hugging me again tightly. "Okay, baby, I believe you."

Ten minutes later, I watched her plane leave the runway and fly into the sky with my heart feeling like it was torn in two.

* * *

My mother hit me up while I was on the way back from the airport saying that she wanted to have a sit down with me and Whitney, and that I should meet her at the beachfront where she was already set up and barbecuing with a few of her coworkers. Even though I didn't really feel like being around anybody, I was thirsty to see Whitney after not talking to her for a couple of days. So, I jetted over so I could see what she was talking about.

When I pulled up, she was just sticking her head inside of the backseat of her truck before pulling out a big bowl of potato salad, handing it to her heavy-set friend who was laughing and saying something to her that I couldn't make out because I was under the air conditioner with my windows rolled up. I parked my car and sat there for a few minutes, overlooking the scenery with a bunch of thoughts running through my head. I knew that I needed to sit down and talk to Whitney, but I didn't know what I was going to say, or how I would react because of her having blocked my number from her phone. I was still hurt by that, and it made me feel angry on so many levels.

My mother must've sensed that I was in the area, because she turned around with a knowing look on her face before walking over to my whip and knocking on the glass. She placed her hand on her hip and waited for me to roll my window down, which I did almost immediately. She leaned forward and placed her forearms on the sill of my car's window. "Uh, I know you don't think that you about to sit yo' ass in this car?" She opened her eyes wide and furrowed her brows.

I shook my head and looked over her shoulder, noting that the beach was packed with women walking around in skimpy bikinis. Boys were in shorts, shirtless, throwing around a football while some of the females were playing volley ball and laughing at each other. My mother had a bunch of her friends section off an area and place four picnic tables together with tablecloths draped over them and all kinds of food. There was also a big barbecue grill smoking right where her friend walked over to. It was how I knew that's where she was set up. I continued to scan the area until I saw Whitney sitting on the bench with her long hair blowing in the wind. Some of it most've went into her mouth because she had it open, pulling a long strand out of it. I didn't know how much I missed her until I saw her right then. That was crazy to me, but I had yet to figure myself out.

I shook my head. "N'all, I don't. To be honest, I was just sitting here trying to figure out what I was going to say to her. I feel like I been messing up ever since she told me she was pregnant. But I don't know how to change, mama. You know I mean well. I just got that street stuff deeply rooted within my soul."

She smiled and reached into the car and rubbed my face. "It's Okay, baby. You're young, and you've never had a man to teach you how to be a man. I mean, I did the best that I could, but I can see that it wasn't enough. However, today can be the start of a whole new life for y'all. I can't allow for you to become one of those deadbeats out there, Jayden. I raised you better than that. So, get out of that car and let's go and talk to my daughter-in-law to be." She laughed when I bugged my eyes at her. "Yeah, that's right, we plotting on yo' ass."

Before I could respond to that, Whitney appeared behind her, with her hair blowing all over her pretty face. We looked eyes before she stepped beside my mother and wrapped her arm around her waist. "Hey, mom. Are you having a hard time over here with him?" She joked, never taking her eyes away from mine.

My mother shook her head. "N'all, he's ready to come out. Ain't you, baby?" She pulled on my door handle, opening it.

I stepped out of the car, and my mother took my hand.

"Now, listen to me, Jayden. You better ignore all of my sex-starved ass friends and focus on Whitney, because she's the reason you're here. Do I make myself clear?" She asked, raising her left eyebrow.

I smiled. "Yeah, I get it."

We walked over to the party, and as soon as I got there, all of my mother's friends were all over me. They were hugging me, kissing my cheeks, and even pressing their fronts into mine. They were so bad that my mother had to pull me away from them, and Whitney looked as if she was on the verge of snapping. Me, personally, I thought it was funny. I just felt like they were older women getting their feel of a younger male. I didn't see no harm in that.

After we finally got through all of that, my mother took Whitney and me away from the party, and had us sit across from each other, while Seagulls flew over our heads, and the rest of the people on the beach enjoyed themselves. She took a deep breath and smiled. "Okay, babies, the reason that I called you two here today is because I want you to get a firm understanding of one another before you leave this beach. You guys are about to be parents. You need each other, and even more than yourselves, your child needs the both of you. Do you understand where I'm coming from?" She asked, looking from Whitney then over to me.

We both nodded, never taking our eyes from her.

"Okay, well, the first thing I want you two to do is to tell the other one how you really feel about them. Don't say anything wrong about them, only say how they make you feel, and be honest. "We'll start with you, Whitney. So, go ahead, baby."

Whitney's eyes bugged out of her head. "Me? Mom, really?"

My mother closed her eyes and nodded. "Yes, go ahead, baby. Get the ball rolling before these mosquitoes start biting."

Whitney nodded, then lowered her head. "I don't know how I feel now. I guess a little angry, but that doesn't stop me from loving you, Jayden, or from thinking about you every second of the day. I haven't even been able to eat because I've been missing you so bad. I wish we could go back to the way things were only a few months back. I wish that you could lay in the bed with me and rub my stomach. I wish that you could go and supply the things that I need for my cravings, whenever they start. I just wish that we could figure this out because being away from you is killing me. I don't know how much more I can take before it becomes a problem for our baby." She looked over to me, and then up to my mother. "I'm done."

My mother reached down and stroked her face. "You're my heart, little girl. I swear I will whoop his ass if he doesn't marry you. I promise, I'm not playing." She turned and glared at me. "Okay, it's your turn, Jayden. Let's see what you got on your Heart. It better be good, too."

I sighed and looked over Whitney's shoulder at a bunch of females that were walking away from the beach with G-strings on. There were three of them, and each one was strapped with their asses jiggling like crazy. I knew I had to focus, but once again my penis was getting the better of me.

Whitney turned around to see what I was looking at and hunched her shoulders inward. "You see, Deb, that's what I'm talking about. How can we ever have anything if his eyes are always wandering to the next female? It makes me feel so freaking insecure, and I know I'm not ugly, but I feel like it because I'm not enough for him." She shook her head and her eyes became watery.

My mother sat beside her and wrapped her arm around her shoulders, mugging me with obvious anger while I sat there feeling like a piece of scum. "There, there, baby. He's just a man, and that's what they do." She kissed her on the side of the forehead. "Don't you worry, we gon' fix all those things that are wrong with him. Now, Jayden, tell this girl how you feel about her and keep your eyes in front of you. Damn. Do you want this girl to lose y'all baby or something?"

I frowned. "Ma, n'all." I leaned over the table and looked Whitney over, even though she wasn't looking at me. "Baby, I'm so sorry. I need you to know that I do love you, and I appreciate you for nourishing our child within your womb. I think about you just as much as you do me, if not more. I been going crazy without you, every single day, I swear." I exhaled and lowered my head. "I think I got a problem or something, because I love the female body way too much. Like it's hard for me to ignore that lower region of myself. I can give you everything that you need and hold you down, but I don't know if I will ever be able to stop chasing other women, or wanting to sleep with them, and I know that sucks to hear, but it's the truth." I raised my head and saw that she still had hers lowered

Now tears were sailing down her cheeks. "I know I'm not the most beautiful girl in the world, Jayden. I know that there are a million girls out there that look better than me and have more of a body than I do. But you know what? None of them will love you as strongly as I will. None of them will love you when you're at your lowest point, and none of them will be the first to give you your first born, but I will. To all of those things, I will. So, even though you make me feel like crap, like I'm not enough, and like all of those women are better than me, I will still always love you, and ride to the ends of the earth for you." She broke into a fit of tears before my mother grabbed her, and allowed for her to sob within her chest. "I just hope that you'll be a good father, Jayden, because I'm not having this baby for me. I'm having it for you, first and for most, because you told me that you'd always be there and that you loved me. It was the only reason I crossed over to you in the first place." She frowned, and tears started to stream down her face even more so.

I reached across the table to grab her hand, taking it within my own. "Whitney, I love you, baby. I swear to God that I do. Please, stop crying. I can't take that. You should know how much I care about you. Damn." I said, feeling my throat get tight.

She shook her head. "No, you don't. You can't. How can you care or love me when you didn't even spend you first night home with me? You spent it screwing your cousin." She said, sounding as if she were running out of breath.

As soon as she said it, I felt like I was about to pass out. My mother popped her neck backward, then gave me a look of shock. "Jayden? I know that ain't true, is it?"

I shook my head. "N'all, we ain't screw that night, but we have since then." I looked across the table at Whitney as she continued to cry, and my mother's face turned beet red.

She looked as if she were ready to jump across the table and whoop my ass, but I didn't care. I had never lied to my mother before in my life, and I wasn't about to start. I respected her more than that.

"Whitney, baby, can you please tell me what you need for me to do? I keep asking you that, but you never say what it is. I'm struggling to understand you and myself right now, so can you please help me out?

I'm begging you." I got up and came around the table, squatting on the left side of her.

The three females from before came and sat down at a picnic table; two over from the one we were at. It didn't take them log before they were all in our mouths, and I didn't care. I just wanted Whitney to feel better. Her being so down was killing my soul. I was willing to do anything.

She took a deep breath and blew it out, then looked down at me. "Honestly, Jayden, I just need for you to leave me alone. You are nowhere near close to being the type of man that I need you to be for myself and our child, when she or he gets here. As long as I allow for you to have this hold on me, you're not going to do anything but slowly kill me, and ultimately our child. I just lost Lincoln not too long ago, and already you're dragging me through the mud. Thanks a lot." She turned to face my mother. "Mama, I love him, but to be with him won't do anything other than break me a part, so I have to let him go, at least until he grows up a little bit. There is too much at stake here, and I am worth more than what he's willing to give me. So, therefore, I have to figure things out on my own, and I'm okay with that." She said with her voice breaking up and tears falling out of her eyes.

"Shit, if she don't want him, I'll take his fine ass any day," said a brown-skinned sista with a fat Cigarillo in her hand. "I guarantee I know what to do with him." She slapped hands with one of her friends before they broke into laughter.

Whitney frowned and looked over her shoulder, mugging the woman that looked to be about nineteen years old. "Excuse you?" She asked, standing up with my mother trying to pull her back down.

The woman laughed and rolled her eyes. "You heard what I said. I didn't stutter." She sucked her teeth loudly and took a hit from her Cigarillo. "You better sit yo' lil' pretty ass down before we come over there and make you." She mugged Whitney and looked her up and down all evil-like.

Whitney shook my mother off her, and before she could grab her, she ran over to the seated woman and swung with wild fists, connecting them one after the other, before grabbing a handful of the woman's hair, slinging her to the ground and kicking her in the face with her Airmax shoe. "You don't know what I been through with him. Bitch, I'll kill you!" She screamed.

One of the other girls grabbed a handful of her hair and yanked her neck backwards. "Bitch, get off of my sister!" She swung and punched Whitney on the side of the head.

I jumped to my feet and got ready to go over there and start knocking hoes out, when my mother kicked off her sandals and rushed the girl that had punched Whitney. She hit her with five quick blows, and the girl took off running with her nose bleeding. The other two was alongside of her, running for their lives.

"Fuck y'all thought this was? Better get up off my baby 'fore I bring this project shit out of me. You better tell 'em, Jayden!" She yelled, picking Whitney up, and wrapping her arm around her.

I took over, bringing her into my embrace while the females hollered from a distance that they would be back, and we'd better be gone. "Mama, you finna pack all this stuff up, and get up out of here. Then, I'm gon' take her home so we can finish talking."

My mother shook her head. "Boy, I ain't finna let them lil'girls ruin my party. If they bring they ass back, then we about to tear this beach up. You should know better than to ask me to do something like that." She waved me off. "But you can take her home though. She don't need to be fighting while she pregnant, even though it look like she can hold her own with no problem." She giggled and hugged Whitney one more time. "You got in her ass, baby. Damn, I love you so much."

Just then, about four of her friends ran over with box cutters in their hands, and their faces full of vaseline as if they were ready to go to war.

"What's up, Deb? You wanna chase they ass down and get it in?" One of the heavier set ones asked, looking down the beach at the fleeting girls.

My mother looked out at them and waved them off. "They don't want them type of problems. If they come back, then we'll show them how we used to get down. But for now, let's just enjoy our party and eat. I'm hungrier than a hostage right now. Take her home, Jayden. Get her off this beach; that's what you can do for me." My mother said, frowning. "And don't think we ain't gon' talk about Myeesha's ass at another time. Hump!"

* * *

On the ride to my mother's house where Whitney was apparently staying for the time being, we didn't say not one word to each other until I pulled up in front of my mother's house. "Aight, I guess this you then. I hope you feel better." I said, feeling sick to my stomach. I didn't want her to get out of the car without us making up, but I was too stubborn to let on, and plus I didn't know what to say to her anyway. All I knew is that I loved her to death, and I didn't know how to handle it.

She took her seatbelt from around her and looked me over closely. "You know, Jayden, I never thought that you'd be the man to make me a statistic. My whole life, whenever I looked up at you, I saw this most amazing person. This handsome man, with all of this swagger. I fell in love with you before I even knew what love really meant because you were always there protecting me and making sure that I was straight. I thought that was so cool, because there aren't many men out here like that. But then, Nico must've seen the yearning for you in my eyes and he told me to stay away from you. That you were no good. That you were rotten, and that all you'd do is fuck me and leave me to the slums. So, he made me promise that I would never go there with you. Made me promise on the love that he and I had for each other that I would never go against his word and screw with you. I promised him, Jayden. I promised him, then broke it the next time I saw you because you are so heavily in my veins. You have this aura about you that draws me to you. You affect me emotionally in a way that I have never felt before, and I am so weak because of this." She shook her head as the tears began to fall again. "You were supposed to be my knight in shining armor. The man that took me away from all of this bull crap that we know as the ghetto of Philly and take me to a place where I could be happy within your arms. You were my fairytale, and with in you I hoped that I would'venever had to grow up." She sighed. "But I have, and within a short period of time, you have made me become an adult. I see you for what you are, and it breaks my heart on so many levels. Still, in all, I love you with all of my heart, and—"

Before she could finish what she was saying, her eyes got as big as saucers, as she looked over my shoulder, opened her mouth wide and covered it with her hand. Then, I saw it too.

Chapter 10

Three niggas with masks covering their faces slid from under the car that was parked in front of mine. Then, two more ran alongside my mother's gangway. Two more came from across the street with assault rifles in their hands, and finally I watched Nico open the door to my mother's house and walk down her steps with a half-mask covering his face. I knew it was him by the way that he walked, and from the eyes. I would never forget how my right hand man's eyes looked in times of war. They were lowered and evil-like.

As soon as he got to the bottom of the stairs, he took a .9 millimeter out of his waistband and jogged around the car to my side. My first instincts were to hit the gas and speed away from the scene, but his guys were standing in front of my car with assault rifles, pointing them directly at me through my driver's side window. Nico came and bumped the man out of the way and upped his gun on me through the glass before cocking his hand back and bringing it forward, shattering my window. *Crash!* The glass splashed all into my lap. Whitney started to scream at the top of her lungs, causing my ears to ring.

"Bitch ass nigga, get the fuck out of the car, right now!" He ordered, trying to open my car door by its handle.

"Ahhhh! Ahhhh! Nico, stop this. Stop this! Please!" Whitney begged him loudly, looking all around in a state of panic.

"Aye, shut the fuck up, sis! This aint got shit to do with you right now! Get the fuck out the car, Jayden! Bitch ass nigga!"

I looked out of my windshield and saw how all of his men had their weapons aimed at me, and I knew that I was trapped. There was no way out of there. Nico was going to kill me if I stepped one foot out of that whip. I knew it was all in his gameplan, so I had to what I had to do.

I grabbed my .45 from off of my waist and put it to Whitney's head, forcing it into her temple, so much so that she had to cock her head all the way to the right. "Nigga, tell them bitch-made muhfuckas to back up right now, or I'mma blow her muthafuckin' head off. This shit ain't sweet. Tell 'em!" I hollered, looking up at Nico, biting on my bottom lip.

I didn't want to have to do what I was, but there was no way I was about to let this nigga leave me in the streets of Philly with my brains all over the pavement. I had to live to fight another day. I knew that nigga loved his sister, regardless to how tough he acted. Whitney and his mother Janet were his life and his weaknesses, just like my mother was mine, and Whitney for the most part, though desperate times called for desperate measures.

Nico took a step back from the car and bucked his eyes. "Nigga, you gon' put a gun to my sister's head? Fuck nigga. You know she pregnant." He shook his head, put his gun tohis temple and hollered. "Ahhh, fuck!" Then, he extended his arm and aimed his pistol back at me. "Nah, nigga, you ain't got that shit in you. You will kill a million niggas, but you ain't 'bout that kind of life." He lowered his eyes again. "You see why I told you to stay away from this punk, Whitney? Now, this nigga got a gun to yo' head, like you one of these hoe ass niggas in the street." He looked over at her.

I pressed the gun harder into her temple, making her head lean further to the side. I was wondering if there were any neighbors that could see what was taking place. The sun was just beginning to set, and our block looked deserted. The way it was in Philly, it could have been a hundred neighbors out on the porch, witnessing it all firsthand, but when the law showed up, they'd still act as if they hadn't seen a damn thing. It was one of the reasons I couldn't understand why all of the sudden Nico had turned bitch and decided to work with the authorities. That wasn't in Philly's DNA.

"Jayden, what are you doing? Please don't kill me." She whimpered.

"Shut up, bitch!" I cocked the hammer on my Forty-Five and mugged Nico with hatred. "Nigga, on my moms, if you don't tell them fuck niggas to get out of my way so I can pull off, I'mma hold court right here and take this bitch with me. Blood in, blood out. You know how this shit go." I sucked my teeth. "Try me."

Nico stuck his arm through the window and put the barrel of his gun to my jaw. "I promise you that you gon' pay for this shit, kid. You done crossed a line that you can never come back from. Mark my words, son, you gon' regret this shit." He stuck his face into the window and spat a loogey on to my jaw before backing up, waving at his men. "Get the fuck out the way. Hurry up!" He stood back from the car and mugged me. "You should've never brought this to family, Jayden. Word is bond."

I threw the car in drive and slowly pulled away from the curb with the gun still pressed against Whitney's jaw, nodding at Nico. "It is what it is, nigga. The war is on. We'll see who survives this shit." I said, feeling my heart beating faster and faster as I sped away from the parking spot.

As soon as I got a safe enough distance down the block, I looked in my rear-view mirror and saw Nico in the middle of the street mugging my whip. I knew that it was about to go down, and the only person I could think about was my mother. I had to get word to her ASAP.

* * *

For some reason, I waited until I was on the highway before I took the gun away from Whitney's cheek. As soon as I did, she slapped me so hard that blood came into my mouth.

"Nigga, don't you ever pull no shit like that! What the fuck is your problem? Huh? What were you thinking?" She yelled.

I frowned and exhaled slowly. "Thinking? I was trying to make sure that I got up out of there alive. That was the only move I could pull. I know Nico crazy about you. He ain't gon' risk me bodying yo' ass. So, I did what I had to." She slapped me again, harder than before. "What if your gun would have gone off, Jayden? What if you would have blown my fucking head off my shoulders, killing me and your baby? Then what, huh? Ahhh, I can't believe you did no shit like that." She ran her hands over her face and slammed her back into her seat, before crying into her hands.

"Man, chill out. Damn, you just looking on the surface. Had I not done what I did, I would have been a dead man. Is that what you want? Huh?" I asked, looking over at her and getting more and more heated. I didn't like nobody putting their hands on me. I didn't care if she was my baby's mother. I mean, I understood that she was pissed, but I felt like she should have seen what we were up against and got with the program. It was all a part of being with a street nigga. I felt like females should've thought that type of shit through a lil' more.

She shook her head. "I should've never crossed them lines with you. I should've listened to my brother. All of this is becuase of me. I had to like you. I couldn't just see you as a brother. N'all, I just had to be me and fuck things up. Now I know for a fact that somebody finna die. My brother ain't finna play with you. I hope you know that." She crossed her arms in front of of her chest, and looked out the windshield, shaking her head.

For some reason her comment sent a major blow to my ego. I mugged her with anger. "Oh, and what you think? I'm gon' just lay down and let this nigga kill me?" I blew air though my teeth. "Yeah, aiight, we'll se about that." I stepped on the gas and headed toward DC with nothing but murder on my mind. I knew one thing, I was going to have to strike Nico and wipe his ass out fast, or it was going to be a major situation. One thing about Philly niggas, when it came to beef, we made sure that our enemies felt it to the max. Me and Nico had grown up deep within the heart of the slums of south Philly. So, we'd been bred to kill with no remorse. I knew I was dealing with an animal, and I was sure he knew the same thing.

"Where are you taking me, Jayden?" She asked calmly, looking over at me.

"Don't worry about it. You coming with me until I can figure this shit out with yo' brother. That's just that. I think it'll be cool if we just sat here in silence for the meantime. I need to collect my thoughts for a lil' while." I reached to my digital dash and turned on some smooth jazz music so I could relax and take it easy. I had to develop a strategy in my mind that would overpower and murder that nigga Nico. I saw how he came with them niggas from the Bronx and it let me know that me and the Shooters had to step our game all the way up.

"Look, Jayden, I don't know who you think you're talking to, or what's going on in your brain, but I want you to get off this highway and let me out. I need to be with my brother right now before he does something stupid over me. I know how to calm him down, and if I don't, then it'll be just like he said. You'll regret it. I don't really think you really know who you're dealing with. That's mind boggling to me. Seriously."

I switched lanes until I was in the express one and mugged her. "Man, fuck yo' brother, Whitney. That nigga can't do shit to me that I can't do to him. You making it seem like he can't be touched or something. Shut yo' ass up, 'cause all you doing is giving me a headache. Fuck!" I said, losing my temper. The whole time I was saying what I was, I wanted to shut up but I couldn't. I was too heated, and I felt like she was choosing Nico over me, and that hurt my heart.

Tears ran down her cheeks. "You know what? Fuck you, Jayden. Fuck you. I'm really starting to hate you. You don't care about me. You never did. All you wanted to do was fuck and piss my bother off in the process. That's it. I wish that I had never been so stupid. I should have never let you run that pretty boy charm on me. I hate this so bad." She lowered her head and screamed into her hands.

"Whitney, I'm begging you. Just be quiet for a second. Save all that emotional shit for another time. Right now, I gotta clear my head, 'cause it's war. War over you. This is what it is." I stepped on the gas and pushed my speeds up to eighty-five miles an hour.

"Take the next exit and let me out of this car, Jayden. I'm not kidding. I've had enough of your bullshit." She said barely above a whisper.

I shook my head. "Nah, you rolling with me. Now, sit back and be quiet. I ain't gon' tell you again." I said, not even looking at her because I was getting so mad.

She unclicked her seatbelt and looked over at me. "Jayden, if you don't get off at the next exit, I'm going to jump out of this car and I don't give a fuck what happen to me or your baby. I'm not kidding." She rolled down her passenger's window as the sun began to set behind the clouds.

"Whitney, stop talking that dumb shit before I kick yo' ass, fa real. You ain't about to do shit. Now, sit back and chill. All that you doing is getting on my nerves because you knew that this was a possibility. We should be trying to figure this all out together. Instead, all you wanna do is cry about it. That ain't gon' solve nothing, now. Damn."

She pulled up the lock on her side and looked over at me. "Jayden, if you don't get off at the next exit, I'm going to jump out of this car and kill me and your baby. I'm not fucking playing around with you. Now I need to be with my brother so I can calm him down. I'm the only one that he will listen to. Let me up out of this car. I don't want to be around you right now. Switch lanes!" She hollered.

Something in me snapped, and instead of switching lanes like she demanded, I sped up the pace and flew past the next exit. "I'm not gon' play these games with you, Whitney. I don't know what you think this is, or if you feel that I'm soft or something, but this ain't that. Now, I told you that you rolling with me until I can figure this whole situation out. So, sit back in yo' seat and chill. I'm not gon' tell you again."

The car sped past the other cars and trucks that were on the road in a blur. I weaved in and out of traffic, driving like a bat out of hell. I was trying to get to DC as soon as possible so I could let my lil' niggas know what was good, and develop a strategy for how we were going to take down Nico and his crew from the Bronx. I wanted to go at them niggas with all that we had. Leave the streets of Philly running red with blood from their bodies. I was so mad that my vision was going hazy.

Whitney looked over at me and smiled. "I hate you, Jayden. I just want you to know that. You are the worst mistake I've ever made in my entire life. I will never understand why you killed Lincoln. I thought it was so you could have me, but now I know it wasn't, and that cut me deep. I could never lay down and give birth to your kid. I can't stand being in this life with you anymore. You made me do this." She opened the door to my car and jumped out of it into traffic, just as a semi truck was speeding down the lane to the right of the one we were in.

"Whitney, noooo!" I hollered, reaching for her, but it was too late.

I watched the semi-truck slam into her, before rolling over her body. Then, it pressed on its brakes, sending smoke from the tires. That made the cars that were behind it slam on their brakes, and before I knew it, there was one crash after the next. I sped over and got off at the next exit, then circled around until I was back along the same place that she'd jumped out of the car. Because of the crashes, it had caused a major traffic jam, so I had to park my car and run about a mile, before I was standing over her mangled form.

She looked like she'd been run over by every last one of the truck's tires, after it smacked her head on. She laid on her back with blood leaking out of her, her eyes were wide open, and I was sure that she was dead, until she blinked and closed her eyes.

I rushed over to her body and kneeled, taking her into my arms, and placing my cheek against her bloody one. Tears ran out of my eyes, and my heart was pounding like an 808 bass drum as I rocked with her "Why, Whitney? Why?" was all I could muster, while people huddled around us until the paramedics came and took her away from me on a stretcher.

* * *

I paced in the hospital's lobby, worrying myself nearly to death and praying that she would pull through. I knew for certain that she had lost a lot of blood, because by the time I got to her, she was lying in a pool of it, so I didn't know how great her chances were of surviving. Before my wait, I was forced to talk to one police officer after the next. They all wanted to know what happened, and what would make her do such a thing. All I could say was the same thing over and over again. I didn't know.

Janet got to the hospital at about one in the morning, and when she saw me waiting in the lobby of the intensive care unit, she ran to me at full speed before wrapping her arms around my neck, and laying her head on my chest. "I told you, baby. I told you to take it easy on her. That she wasn't well. Now look what has happened. Look at where my baby is now." She sobbed, crying uncontrollably into my chest while I rubbed her back, and held her as tight as I could without hurting her.

"I'm sorry, mama. I swear it wasn't my fault. She just said that she couldn't take this life no more." I felt the tears running down my cheeks as I imagined the semi-truck running over Whitney, and then the after effect of her laying in the middle of the highway, mangled, and barely alive.

I knew it was all my fault, and I didn't know what to do or what to say. I thought about our child inside of her belly, and my knees got weak. So much so that

I buckled while holding Janet, and we fell to the ground crying in each other's arms, holding one another tighter and tighter.

I heard ths sounds of tennis shoes squeaking on the floor, looked up and saw Nico rushing over to us with an evil mug on his face. "Bitch ass nigga. I'm a kill you!" he hollered, running full speed.

Janet broke our embrace and stood up, blocking his path by wrapping her arms around him. "Nico, baby, don't do this here. Please, you're on bail. They can hit you with bail jumping and put you right back in prison. Come on now. Please, son." She cooed to him while holding him as best she could.

I could see the veins popping out of his neck as he looked me over. I slowly made my way to my feet with my upper lip curled. "Yo, I ain't have nothing to do with this, Nico. She said she was tired of living, man. I tried to grab her arm, but she jumped anyway." I stepped forward, and as soon as I did, he acted like he wanted to knock his mother down to get to me.

Honestly, I felt like banging that nigga right there. Even though Nico was a killer, he couldn't fuck with my hands and he knew it. We'd fought many times before and he always came out on the losing end. Physically, he was no match, and I really felt like taking my anger out on his punk ass in that moment.

"This is yo' fault, nigga. You put a gun to my lil' sister's head. You did this. You probably pushed her out of that car, knowing your grimey ass. I should beat the fuck out of you!" He growled.

I sucked my teeth. "What's hannin', den?" I stepped closer, tired of playing games with his bitch ass and wanting to see him bleed by my own doing. I was hurting over Whitney and needed to take it out on somebody.

He pushed his mother away from him and started in my direction. I cocked back and swung, hitting him right on his chin, turning him sideways before he fell to the ground unconscious. Janet's eyes were wide open, and the other people that were sitting in the waiting room got up and ran. I jumped over Nico's body and bounced out of the hospital with my heart bleeding heavily for Whitney.

Chapter 11

I bowed my head and tooted up the two lines of Percocet that I'd crushed up. I had a blunt in one hand and a bottle of Hennessy in the other one, trying to run away from the pain inside of my heart, but neither antidote was working for me because I still felt like I was being ripped in two.

It was two days later, and Whitney was still in the hospital, fighting for her life. I wanted to be by her side so bad. I was missing her and yearning for her presence. I couldn't stop crying, and I hated that part of myself because I felt so weak and emasculated. I wished that I could go back and change everything. Had I been able to, I would have never crossed the lines with her in the first place. I would have kept everything on the up and up and protected her and Janet like Nico had previously asked me to.

"Say, kid, you can sit on that couch and toot that shit all day, but it ain't gon' make you feel no better. You gotta get out there and kill something. It's the only remedy." Naz said, tilting the bottle of Hennessy up and swallowing like he was hella thirsty. He licked his lips and tried to stand up, staggering on his feet. "Yo, I'm about to go upstairs and get some sleep. You can stay down her and get your mind right and take as long as you need to. Poppa supposed to be stopping by to drop off some cash, and he say he need to holler at you about something. Just giving you a heads up. I'll rap with you in the morning. Love, son." He staggered to the stairs and took them one by one as slowly as he could. He looked like he was fucked up, and smelled even worst.

As soon as he left, I dropped to my knees and broke into a fit of tears over Whitney. I pulled out my phone so I could see her pictures. That beautiful face, that body, and I imagined how she felt in my arms. It was killing me to know that she may never be there again. I needed her with every passing second.

I could hear Naz and his baby mother, Shawn, arguing upstairs. A few minutes later, she appeared at the bottom of the steps, looking me over, and I didn't even notice until I looked up.

I tried to wipe my face clean as she walked over to me with a concerned look on her face.

"Jayden, baby, what's the matter?" She asked, sitting on the couch beside me.

Shawn and I had went to school together, and back in the day we were a couple for a time. That was before we drifted apart, and I wound up hooking her up with my cousin Naz after he moved over from New York. Since then, Shawn and I had just been real cool. When Naz dropped the ball, I went behind his back to make sure that his baby mother and child were well taken care of. I'd already paid up all their bills for two years. I made sure that every time I saw Shawn that I gave her no less than five bands. I just felt like I owed her for hooking her up with such a loser. Plus, I cared for her and my lil' cousin.

I lowered my head and shook it. "It's Whitney. She tried to commit suicide and it's killing me right now because I know it was mostly my fault. I don't know if she gon' make it." I said with my voice breaking up. I felt the tears running down my cheeks again. I wiped them away and on to the legs of my Gucci denims. Taking a deep breath, I tried to get a hold of myself as best I could.

Shawn wrapped her arm around my shoulder and pulled me so that my head was lying on her breasts. She was wearing a plain white T-shirt and a pair of shirts that I couldn't see because the shirt was so long. "I'm so sorry to hear that, Jayden, but I'm pretty sure it wasn't your fault. Maybe she was battling a severe case of depression. Sometimes you can't really tell until it's too late." She rooked me back and forth with my head laying on her breasts.

For the first time since the whole incident had happened, I started to feel a little better, and I was secretly thankful that she had come down the stairs. I cried harder and harder, thinking about Whitney. I kept on seeing images of her in my mind. Somewhere she was smiling, and otherwhere she was crying over something I had done. It was killing me worse than ever. I just wanted her back, safe and sound. It was all my fault. I felt like the worst nigga in the whole wide world. For some reason, I got to shaking badly.

"Aww, baby, it's going to be okay," Shawn whispered, then put her right thigh over me so she could wrap her arms around me more firmly. Then, she wiped away my tears and kissed my cheek with her juicy lips. "It's okay, Jayden. I'm here. I'm here for you and I ain't going nowhere." She kissed my lips, and then sat back and looked into my eyes, wiping my tears away as they came out of my eyes with her thumbs.

I don't know if it was the liquor. Or maybe it was the pills. But for some reason, my dick was harder than it had ever been, and she got to looking like Whitney to me. Her shirt was matted to her titties from the water I'd cried on to them, and I could clearly make out both of her brown nipples. That turned me on so bad that I couldn't stop myself from doing the next thing that I did.

I leaned forward and kissed her lips, sucking them into my mouth. Then, I ran my hands underneath her shirt, taking her breasts into my hands and squeezing them together while she tongued me down with her eyes closed. She was moaning into my mouth and humping into my hard dick.

"It's okay, Jayden. You can have me. Just hurry up before Naz wakes up. Hurry up and fuck me real quick. I'll heal you, baby." She whispered, unbuckling my belt and squatting so she could pull my pants down my ankles.

As soon as they were there, she drug my boxers down next, pulled her shorts down and off her ankles, finally straddling me and opening her sex lips. She forced my big dick head into her tight ass pussy, rocking forward on it.

"Fuck, fuck, fuck. Oooh, shit, fuck, Jayden, fuck, Jayden. Oooh, wee." She moaned, rocking into me faster and faster with her head tilted backward.

I sucked her titties through her shirt before pulling it all the way up, exposing them, then attacking her hard nipples. Because she was still breast feeding their son, her milk oozed out of the tips of her and ran down to her stomach. I tried to lick up as much as I could and that seemed to turn her all the way on. She got to fucking me so fast that the couch was moving backward. I squeezed her breasts in my hand, forcing more of her liquid out.

"Play with my titties, Jayden. Play with 'em. Unn, un, un, un, un, uhhh, un. It's. Unn, uhh. You so deep. You. So deep. Fuck!" She hollered, holding on to my shoulders and bouncing on me faster and faster with her head tilted backward.

I grabbed her ass and held it in my hands, squeezing and feeling its softness. Whitney flashed in and out of my mind, causing tears to run down my cheeks. Then, I was coming deep within her womb.

"Uhhh, uhhh, I'm cuming, Jayden. I'm cuming." She moaned, humping me faster and faster until she started to shake uncontrollably. She was licking all over my neck, ending in it a bunch of shudders.

There was a loud *voom!* I looked over my shoulder to see Poppa drop two duffle bags on each side of him. He had a frown on his face as he looked at the both of us.

Shawn slowly climbed off my lap and pulled her shirt down. She then picked up her shorts, sliding them up her body. There were two big wet stains in front of her shirt from where milk was constantly coming out of her. She remained silent and crept up the stairs, slightly nudging Poppa on her way past him.

Poppa looked up the stairs at her until she disappeared, then shook his head. "Bitches ain't shit." He picked up the bags and walked over to me, dropping them by the couch. "Yo, what was all that about?" He asked, mugging me.

I finished getting myself together, then shrugged. "I don't know, bruh. I'm just fucked up right now. What's in the bag?" I asked, buckling my belt.

He looked me over for a long time, curling his upper lip. "Yo, you know we don't get down like that, big homey. That shit was shysty as hell. You fucking your cousin's baby mother. What type of shit is that?" He asked, wiping his mouth with his hand.

I slid my pistol from under the couch and put it back on my hip. I didn't feel like explaining nothing to him right then. I was already feeling like shit for fucking her. Then, on top of that, I was missing Whitney at the same damn time. "Yo, we'll holler about that later. Now, what's in the bags?" I asked, looking into his eyes.

He sucked his teeth and waved me off. "Yeah, aiight, nigga. Well, we definitely gon' have to talk. But for now, I need you to handle some business with me. I got five hundred thousand in them bags so I can cop this work from my niggas out in Virginia. We gon' meet them out side of the Waffle House over on the Avenue in like ten minutes. After that, me and you need to talk. Word is bond." He shook his head.

I stood up and grabbed all of my things, getting myself together. "Yeah, let's do that, and I'm asking you to keep this between us, for now. At least until you hear my side of the story."

He picked up the two big bags and laughed. "Yeah, there is always two sides to every story. Your side, her side, and the real side. That's the one I saw. I watched y'all fucking like y'all had plenty of practice. That couldn't have been the first time."

I could still taste Shawn's milk on my tongue. For some reason that caused my piece to throb. I didn't know what was wrong with me, but I had to figure it out real soon.

* * *

Poppa pulled the Navigator to the side of the road and looked down at his phone as cars continued to fly down the busy street. He frowned as he read the text. "Fuck, now these niggas saying they gon' be a lil' late." He sucked his teeth and texted back to whoever he was communicating with. He then put his phone back into his lap and pulling back into traffic.

Meek Mill's "Dream Chasers" played out of his speakers. The bass caused the back of my head to vibrate. "Yo, how long they saying they gon' be, kid?" I asked, puffing on a Dutch stuffed with Syracuse Hydro.

"Saying we can meet up at the same spot in like an hour. I wanna go and get something to eat anyway, and you can tell me what's good with you and Naz's baby mother. That's still throwing me for a loop. Where is your loyalty?" He asked, looking over at me. His entire dashboard was lit up. It looked like a spaceship command center or something. The lil' homey had come a long way since we'd started hustling together. It let me know that I had to step my game up, after I bodied Nico of course.

I shrugged. "Yo, it really just happened. I was on some drunk shit. Shorty was consoling the kid, and one thing led to another. Next thing I knew, we were coming together, and I was feeling like shit." I puffed on the blunt and tried to hand it to the homey.

He pushed my hand away and shook his head. "Nah, son, that ain't looked like you regretted that at all. Shorty was riding you like a jockey, and you was gripping her backside and everything. I can't believe you'd stoop so low. You and that nigga Naz are cousins and day-ones. Kid gon' flip when you tell 'em, and he gon' kick that bitch out. I know that for a fact. The homey already half off his rocker." He shook his head. "I can't smoke behind a traitor. We got a get an understanding with the homey first, and then we can jam the way we need to. When do you wanna have a sit down and clear the air?" He asked, taking a Dutch from out of a cup holder, putting it in his mouth, then lighting it.

I nodded. "On some real shit. We should holler at bruh as soon as we done handling this business."

I ain't want none of that shit hanging over my head anyway. I felt like I needed to holler at Naz, tell him what it was, and get it over with. Then, we could focus in on Nico, but just thinking about how it would go down with my cousin got me to having the bubble guts. On top of that, I had to piss bad as hell.

"Nah, we gon' probably have to holler at the homey in the morning. He was fucked up when he let me in. We'll catch him after breakfast or something, get an understanding, and keep it moving. I'm curious to see what he wanna do."

"Yo, I gotta piss badder than a muhfucka, kid. Pull into that alley over there before I flood your seats." I said, squeezing my thighs together. I felt like my bladder was about to burst.

Poppa laughed, making the right turn into the alley. "That's what you get for fucking your cousin bitch, nigga. You better hope that shit don't burn." He said, driving into the middle of the alley and parking his truck.

The alley had about ten stray cats inside of it. They jumped out of the big garbage can as soon as his big truck pulled up. The alley lights had been shot out, and it was so dark that the cat's eyes were different shades of electric green.

"Piss like a river, my nigga. Then, we about to go and get some Gyros." He leaned forward to change the CD, after pressing power on the dash, puffing on the big Dutch in his mouth.

Boo-wa! Boo-wa!

I'd slammed the barrel of my gun to his temple and pulled the trigger, blowing his brains against the driver's window. His head fell forward and landed on the horn, blaring it loudly. The cats took off running in every direction. I reached across his body and opened the driver's door and pushed him out of it. Then, I jumped out and ran around to his side, grabbed one of his arms and pulled him until he was up against the big metal garbage can. I squatted and took everything out of his pockets, turning them inside out, trying my best to make it look like a robbery.

Then, I stood up, and looked down on him with my gun extended. "Fuck nigga!" *Boo-wa! Boo-wa! Boo-wa!* The fire from my gun lit up the alley again and again.

I ran back to his truck and removed the duffle bags, threw them on my shoulders after wiping down the insides of his truck and broke down the alley.

Chapter 12

I'd only met Poppa's mother three times in my life, and each time she always made me feel welcome to her home, even though me and Poppa never stayed there for more than fifteen minutes. Usually we'd come in and he'd have me sit on the couch while he ran upstairs and got dressed or put a certain amount of money in his safe, or something. He had his own crib that he shared with his daughter and baby mother, but like me, he felt that the safest place to keep his most valuable possessions were at his mother's crib, as most cats in Philly did. But I said that to say that I felt weird holding her while we sat in the front row of the church at Poppa's funeral.

She couldn't stop from breaking down repeatedly. She was sobbing loudly, falling off the bench while I tried to hold her up with very little success. I looked up just as Kilroy walked up to the casket and placed a bottle of Ace of Spades on his chest and kissed him on the forehead. Naz held Shawn's hand with dark shades on his face, but I'd seen him more than once dab with a tissue under the glasses before fixing them on his face. Shawn rubbed his shoulders as their son kicked his little legs in the carrier beside her.

Poppa's mother laid her face into the crux of my neck and hollered that she wanted Jesus to take her away. That she missed her baby already. All I could do was hold her as tight as I could and continue to give her as much support as my heart would allow, especially when the choir got up and began to perform a selection for the church, while the Pastor, a heavy-set, dark skinned man, nodded and fanned himself with one of the paper makeshift fans that the ushers had passed out to the entire church.

As Poppa's mother cried in my arms, I wondered why I didn't feel any remorse for killing him. Maybe it was because I knew that if Naz had found out that I fucked his baby mother that we would have been in a war alongside the one that I'd already waged against Nico. I knew that my cousin was a savage. He'd probably blow his baby mother's head off and then bam the kid next before coming for me.

Naz was one of those psychotic types that didn't understand that you couldn't go around killing people just because you wanted to. Had he found out about me and Shawn, I would've had to kill him for sure. That could've been one of the reasons I felt no remorse for killing Poppa. Maybe it was the fact that I was now $500,000 to the good, and nobody knew anything about it. I had plans of relocating out of Philly, and the money would help me when the time came. Ever since I'd been warring with Nico, I hadn't been able to hustle as hard as I needed to, and the one thing I hated was losing out on money, so the death of Poppa had benefited me financially as well. Far as I was concerned, it was just business.

Poppa's mother began to cry harder as the choir bellowed their rendition of "I Shall Wear a Crown". She started to shake in my arms. Finally, I let her go and she fell to the capret carpet, rolling around on it with her black dress flying up. I was over it. I didn't have any more empathy to share with her. Two of the Shooters came over and helped her back to the bench.

I walked over and sat down beside Naz, leaning into his ear. "Yo, you already know we can't let this shit ride, my nigga. We gotta put on for the lil'homey, find them Virginia niggas and bam they ass. Word is bond." I said, curling my lip like I had a habit of doing. I looked past him and down to Shawn's thick thighs that were crossed in her black Burberry dress that I'd bought her for the occasion.

She looked up at me and lowered her eyes before blinking the right one. It made my dick stir because I was pretty sure that she knew what I'd done.

Naz sucked his teeth. "You already know we gon' put on for the homey. Don't nobody cross the Shooters and live to tell about it. Them niggas gon' get ttheirs, right after we handle Nico. It look like the Mexican Posse gon' be clapping back too. Word on the street is that they're calling in reinforcements from their homeland. I don't know when its gon' go down, I just know that it is. We gotta be ready." He wrapped his big arm around Shawn possessively and exhaled.

Just then I saw Kilroy walking over to where we were seated. He stopped and gave an older lady a hug, kissed her on both cheeks then started to squeeze through the people that were seated at our pew before sitting beside me. "Yo, we gotta get over to your mother's crib, Boss. Some of the Shooters say they been beating on her door and she aint answering, and haven't for the last ten minutes, even though her truck parked in front of the house. I don't know what's going on, but we gotta move out."

Naz stood up and almost knocked Shawn over. "I'm rolling, too. From now on, I wanna know everything that's taking place with our mob. We taking too many L's and I ain't with this shit."

I didn't know what the fuck he was talking about other than Poppa's murder, but I wasn't trying to hear that shit. I jumped up and ran toward the back of the church where the doors were, and ran out into the pouring rain, just as lightning flashed across the sky and thunder rumbled. Kilroy was right behind me, along with Naz who staggered at the top of the steps.

Lightning flashed across the sky again, and the raindrops began to drench me before I could even make it fully down the stairs of the church, praying silently in my mind that my mother was okay.

"Aw, shit, it's a muthafucking hit, bruh. Watch out!" Kilroy yelled, coming from out of his waistband with two .45 automatics.

I don't know how I missed them, but I had. I looked down and across the street, just as the side door to the brown van slid to the side, and out jumped two armed men with black ski masks over their faces and assault rifles in their hands. *Boom-boom-boom-boom-boom-boom-boom-boom.* Their bullets slammed into the body of the church right beside me, knocking paint off its exterior, and causing sparks to fly into the air.

"Shit!" I ducked and ran back into the church as more and more bullets were popped in our direction.

Kilroy remained outside, bussing his guns, clapping back at the Shooters like a gangsta. I ducked behind the church door, pulled my .45 out of my waist and bussed out the front window of the church, bussing back at the van. *Bocka, bocka, bocka, bocka.* My bullets crashed through the church's window again and again. All the church goers behind me where murmuring and ducking for cover. Some screamed and begged for the Lord to save them. It sounded like utter chaos until the van screeched its way down the street and disappeared.

I ran and opened the door, running back outside into the rain, as Kilroy ran down the street, bussing his gun at the fleeting van.

Naz laid with his back up against the church's sign, holding his stomach. Blood leaked through his fingers as he winced in pain with the rain beating down on his dark colored face. Beside him was his .45. "Yo, I'm hit, kid. Help me get in the car before Twelve get here." He groaned, reaching up for me.

Kilroy came running down the street with a crazy look on his face. "That was them Mexicans, kid. No doubt, that's the same van they always had. It's war now, fuck this shit. The homey aight?" He asked, dropping to his knees beside us.

About ten of the Shooters ran out of the church and surrounded us with guns in their hands. I wanted to holler at the lil' niggas and ask them where they had been when we were under attack, but I didn't want to waste my breath.

Naz handed me his car keys. I took them and jogged to his whip, opened the backdoor then ran back over to him. "Aiight, y'all, get him up and put him in the car. Hurry up 'cause I can hear sirens." I said, running to my own car. There was no way I was finna get caught up with them niggas. I had to get to my mother's crib. I didn't care if I had to go alone.

After they loaded Naz into the backseat of his car, Kilroy jogged over to me. "Come on, boss, they gon' take the homey to the hospital. We gotta go make sure your mother is okay."

* * *

By the time we pulled up to my mother's crib, it was raining so bad that it felt like rice was hitting my car. I parked it along the curb and ran up the steps, taking them two at a time before putting my key into the lock, and turned it, pushing the door in. Kilroy was right behind me with his pistol out, along with four of the Shooters.

"Mama! Mama! Wher you at?" I yelled, running in and straight toward the stairs that led to her bedroom.

I'd run past the television as it blared loudly in the living room. On it was The Real House Wives of Atlanta, and they were on the screen arguing about something. I climbed the steps, running straight to her bedroom, finding it empty, then came down the hall, opening one door after the next. First the linen closet, then the guest bedroom's door. Both were empty. I continued to make my way down until I got to the bathroom door. I opened that one and looked inside. Once again, it was empty. My mother was nowhere to be found.

"Ay! Jayden, down here, bruh! Aw, shit, this ain't right!" I heard Kilroy say, and my heart began to pound in my chest as I ran down the stairs, nearly falling.

"Where you at?" I hollered.

"In the kitchen. It's fucked up, bruh. She dead." He said loud enough for me to hear him.

I jogged past the living room and the television again, and into the kitchen where Kilroy stood with his head down. When he felt my presence, he stood to the side so I could see what he was looking at.

There was my mother, laid on here back with her throat slit from one ear to the next. Her blood was all over the kitchen. Most of it was already dried up which let me know that she'd ben dead for a long time. That and the fact that her body was bloated. She looked like she was seconds away from popping, and the stench coming from her was so bad that the Shooters were gagging all around me. There were a thousand roaches crawling all over her body.

I dropped to my knees and pulled her into my arms as the roaches crawled up my arm and into the sleeve of my shirt. I didn't even care. I couldn't believe that my precious mother was gone. The tears sailed down my cheeks and my heart felt like it wanted to stop beating.

"This Nico's work, ain't it, bruh?" Kilroy asked, shaking his head.

I rocked back and forth with my mother, crying with her head against my chest. I couldn't believe that she was gone. I could not believe that Nico could stoop so low as to target my mother, after I could have killed Janet a long time ago, though that thought had never crossed my mind. I preferred to go at him like a man, not through the women in our lives like a bitch.

"Yo, Jayden, we gotta get out of here man. Unfortunately, she dead, bruh. We gotta regroup; get our minds together." Kilroy said.

I picked my mother's head up so that the open mouth in her throat closed just a bit. Her body was twice its normal size, bloated as rigor mortis started to set in some time ago. I leaned down and kissed her forehead, slowly laid her on her back down, then stood up, nodding. "This Nico's work for sure. He's the only one that knew where my mother stayed." I wiped the tears from my face and took a deep breath after grabbing my pistol from the kitchen floor. I felt the roaches crawling all over my arms and neck. I shook my shirt to discard them, then jumped up and down to try and get rid of the rest.

"Aiight then, I say we go at that nigga full fledge then. All or nothing. We end this war once and for all so we can get at them Mexicans. We can't take none of this lying down. I refuse to." Kilroy said, walking out of the kitchen.

* * *

Even though I was ready to go to war with Nico, because of what he had done to my mother, physically I was in no position to do so, because as soon as we made it back to our trap in DC, I fell to my knees at the door and threw up all over the floor before I broke down crying my eyes out over my mother. It wasn't the kind of crying that females and babies did either. N'all, I'm talking that cry of a goon. I fell to my knees and the water gushed out of my eyes, though I kept my mouth shut. My whole body felt like it was exhausted, and I could barely move a muscle. I kept on shaking like crazy, and every time I tried to get up from my knees, I would grow weak and fall back down until the homies came over and helped me get to the couch.

Once there I laid my head in my lap and continued to let my emotions come out of me until I was able to get a hold of myself, and that's when my phone buzzed. I picked it up and saw that it was Nico's number. Before I could even think to do anything differently, I answered the call and put it to my ear. "So, we killing mothers now?" I asked, trying to catch my breath because my heart was beating so fast.

Nico laughed. "I mean, why not? You killed one. An eye for an eye, muthafucka. You know what it is. Philly's law of the land."

I closed my eyes. "I never even thought about killing your mother, Nico. I'd never do no shit like that. I love her just like I loved my own." I said, breaking up at the last part.

"I ain't talking about my muthafucking mama! I'm talking about my sister, nigga. She died two days ago, and it's yo fault, bitch nigga. How the fuck you saying you look at my mother like your own when you was fucking her?" He hollered into the phone.

I could hear the sound of guns being cocked and loaded in the background. He coughed and then sucked his teeth loudly. My heart skipped a beat, and then I felt like I could no longer breathe. Had he just told me that Whitney had passed away? And if so, why had nobody told me? At the very least, his mother Janet could have. It felt like the room was spinning around me.

I dropped to my knees beside the couch and took one deep breath after the next. "You saying that

Whitney died, Nico, on some real shit?" I asked with my voice breaking up.

He sucked his teeth. "Nigga, you acting like you gave a fuck. You ain't care about my sister, nigga. You a selfish type of nigga. You don't give a fuck about nobody but yo' muthafucking self. It's always been that way. But it's good. I'm ready to end this shit once and for all. You down for that?" He asked, then grew silent, I imagined waiting for my response.

I was so hurt over hearing that Whitney had died, that for a second the last thing that he'd said to me really didn't register for a minute. I was on my knees with tears of anger rolling down my cheeks. I kept on seeing first my mother's face and then Whitney's. I couldn't believe that in just a matter of hours, in my mind, that I'd lost both women. It was almost too much for me to bare.

"Bitch nigga, did you hear what the fuck I said?" Nico hollered into the phone, sounding like he spat all over it.

"Fuck that nigga talking about, Jayden? Word is bond, just ask him where he is and we can handle this shit in the slums, the Philly way, nah'mean." Kilroy said, cocking his M-4 and pacing, looking me over.

I slowly stood up on weak knees and exhaled loudly. "What you wanna do, Nico? Let's nip this shit in the bud."

"Yo, on some real shit nigga, we can fight it out to the death, right at Wilson's gym. Get in the ring and beat each other sensless until nobody gets up. I'm 'bout that life if you are, nigga. Fuck these guns. We can put these bitches down and handle business like real gangstas. You feel me?"

At that point, I just wanted to get my hands on Nico in any way that I could. I knew I was going to kill him one way or the other. There was no way around it. I didn't mind fighting him to the death, even though it sounded like a setup. If this nigga was talking about fighting with our fists, then why in the fuck was I hearing his goons loading up their weapons as if they were preparing to go to war with Trump? I nodded and laughed to myself. I had to outthink Nico. Just get him into the vacinity of where I needed him to be, and once there, I could knock his head off and punch out his light, as we say in Philly.

"Nigga, I'll meet you at Wilson's gym, and we can get it in until your heart stop, fuck nigga. You know what it is with my hands. It ain't sweet, so let's get it. When you trying to do this?"

Kilroy's phone buzzed, and I watched him look down at it before his eyes were as wide as an open garage door. "Aw, fuck, blood. I gotta get to the crib. Them bitch ass Mexicans done shot my shit up!" He hollered, frowning at his phone.

I could hear Nico laughing on the phone. "Sound like y'all got problems. You better handle that first, then get at me. I'll meet you at Wilson's on Friday at one in the morning. Be there, bitch nigga. That's if you ain't scared to be. And don't worry about my niggas airing you fuck boys out. Long as y'all keep that shit on some fist-fighting shit, that's where it'll remain. But if we smell any type of bull, then we gon' pump so many bullets into yo' fags that it's gon' look like yo' whole crew doing the Floss, all at one time." He laughed into the phone before hanging it up.

Chapter 13

Kilroy took his baby mother into his arms and hugged her tightly, kissed her on the cheek, then bent down and wrapped his arms around his crying daughter before picking her up and rubbing her back. Me and the Shooters stood around with mugs on our faces. It was an hour after he'd received the text that his crib had been shot up by the Mexican Posse. After the Shooters had rushed into his crib and got his daughter and baby's mother to safety, they whisked them off to his grandmother's crib over on Parker Place, which is where we were.

"Are you sure it was a brown van?" Kilroy asked his baby's mother while he bounced his daughter, trying to console her as best he could.

Her little face was the shade of red, tears dripped off her chin, and snot ran out of her nose. I could tell that she was traumatized, and it broke my heart. I was tired of the women in our crews being preyed upon. I was ready to kill up some shit before I left for Atlanta.

Me and Myeesha had already spoken, and she'd pushed our date back an additional two weeks so I could finish up my business in Philly. She understood and said that it would give her more time to perfect the move, which I was glad to hear, though she was extremely devastated when finding out that my mother had been killed.

Kilroy's baby's mother nodded furiously. "Baby, I was sitting on the porch with her when they rolled up and opened the side door. I saw three yellow dudes with real curly, jet black hair. As soon as I did,

I grabbed her little hand and we ran back inside of the screen door, just before they started shooting for a full minute. The inside of our home has been ripped to shreds. What they didn't destroy, the police did. I don't understand why we have to go through this. Your daughter and I are innocent. You said that niggas in Philly never crossed the females, or the children, so why are they doing it now?" She yelled, making their daughter scream at the top of her lungs.

Once again, it made me feel some type of way because no baby should've been traumatized like she had been. It made me hate the Mexican Posse and Nico's bitch ass. *What type of real men preyed on babies?* I thought.

Kilroy held the back of his daughter's head and kept her close to his chest. "Yo, Chelsey, stop all that hollering. You're scaring our baby." He mugged her and kissed his daughter. "It's okay, mama. Daddy's here, baby, and everything is going to be alright." He kissed her cheek and continued to bounce her while I got madder and madder.

Chelsey scrunched her face and shook her head. "What are you going to do, Kilroy? I can't even think straight knowing that there are men out there trying to kill us for no good reason. It's not fair. I don't know what you're doing in those streets, but obviously you're fucking up and it's falling on our shoulders. You need to get your shit together." She said, walking into his face, pointing her finger at him.

He frowned and mugged her before looking down at his daughter. He took two steps to his right and handed her over to me. She looked as if she were on her way to sleep, so as he handed her to me, she reached until she was safe in my arms. As soon as she was, I began to bounce her while I rubbed her small back. She couldn't have been no older than two years old.

"Yo. Take her over there for a second, Jayden. Word is bond."

I walked backward while holding her close to my chest. Just feeling her there made me feel some type of way. I started to think about Whitney and our baby that had been growing inside of her. I'd always wanted a daughter of my own. One that I could cherish and spoil all of her life. Now that I'd lost my mother and Whitney, I wanted a daughter worst than ever.

Before I could get out of the living room where we'd all been, I watched Kilroy grab his baby's mother by the throat and slam her into the wall, before lifting her off of her feet. "Bitch, didn't I tell you about your mouth and how you speak around my daughter? Huh?" He asked her through his clenched teeth.

I could tell that he was squeezing her neck harder and harder because her eyes were bugged out of her head and she kept on hitting at his hand around her throat while her legs kicked wildly.

I turned my back to them so that his daughter wouldn't be able to see what was going on. A major part of me wanted to go back in there and get him up off of her, but my emotions were running high, and it had not been that long ago that the homey had lost Poppa and a few other members of the Shooters. I felt like Chelsey had picked the wrong time to come at him with that bullshit. Though I didn't condone what he was doing to her, I didn't feel like it was my place to break that shit up and risk beefing with the only true, loyal savage I had on my team.

"Answer me, bitch!" He snarled before letting his hold loose enough for her to talk.

She fell to her feet, coughing and still trying to get his hand from around her throat. "I'm sorry, Kilroy, damn. You ain't gotta do me like this. I'm just scared." She cried, trying to wrap her arms around him.

He pushed her into the wall and grabbed a handful of her hair, placing his nose against hers. "Bitch, if I ever have to tell you this shit again, word is bond, I'ma kick yo' ass for an hour straight before I drop yo' ratchet ass back off in Brooklyn. Now, I got too much shit on my plate to be out here playing games with you. You knew I was a street nigga before you rotated down this way. Get yo' shit together and let me handle mine. You understand me?" He asked, mugging her.

She nodded as he let her go so she could wrap her arms around his body. "Yes, daddy, I'm sorry. Please don't send me back to Brooklyn. I wanna be here with you. I'm sorry." She hugged him tightly and cried into his chest.

Meanwhile, I bounced their daughter just enough to help her to fall asleep. I felt so whole with her in my arms. It was an unexplainable feeling that I'd never thought could ever happen. I felt like I was catching Baby Fever.

* * *

"You see these niggas wanna play games, not knowing that I know where they bitches be. I tried my best to keep this shit in the streets amongst us men, but a muhfucka always gotta take the kid's kindness for weakness." Kilroy said as he finished wrapping the duct tape around the last Mexican female's wrists and dropping the tape back into his knap sack. Afterward, he took out his .45 and cocked it.

I felt my stomach turn upside down as I stood about five feet away from him in the Catholic Church's basement, two days after Kilroy's crib had been shot up by the Mexican Posse. Not only did the homey have nine of the women tied up, but he also had the Shooters and myself tie up about eleven kids. I felt super guilty and a little unsure about all of this.

He wiped his mouth with the same hand he was holding his gun with, then extended it and placed the barrel to Pablo's wife's forehead and cocked the hammerr before ripping the tape from her mouth. "Bitch, you're Pablo's wife, am I right?" He asked, pressing the barrel even harder into her skin.

She curled her upper lip. "Yeah, so what? Why are you here, you fucking monkey?" She spat, looking into his eyes. Her response blew my mind. I was not expecting no shit like that. I thought she would start to cry like most women would have. Kilroy looked over at me with his eyes bucked before turning to face her. "Bitch, you think you tough, huh? You ready to die, or you gon' tell me where the Mexican Posse's headquarters is? It's your choice." He said, forcing the gun harder into her forehead so bad that her skin was turning red around the barrel. He wrapped her long hair into his fist.

She continued to look him in the eyes. "Fuck you. Do what you gotta do. I'll never tell on my family." She spat into his face and closed her eyes.

Kilroy released her hair and wiped his face, looking down on her in disbelief. "Bitch!" *Boom.*

Her head jerked violently on her shoulder as the back of it exploded and shot her brains against the church's white walls. Then, what was left of her head fell to her lap. The smell of brain and gun powder entered the air.

He stepped one foot to the left of her and ripped the tape off another female's mouth, taking the hot barrel of his gun and shoving it into her eyesocket. "Where are the Mexican Posse's headquarters? You got one chance to tell me."

"Our Father, who art in Heaven, hallow be thy name. Thy Kingdom come, may thy will be done, on earth as it is done in Heaven."

Boom! His bullet slammed into her eyesocket, blowing the right side of her face off. She fell sideways in her chair before bleeding out on the floor.

The next female would keep her silence as well, and just like the other two, he would blow her head off. I felt like he was going to make his way down the line of women, and all of them were going to do the exact same thing. All until I looked down the line and saw the Priest with tears running down his old and wrinkled, face. He shook his head, hollering into the duct tape with his eyes closed tightly. I walked over to him and ripped away the duct tape from his mouth.

"Thirty-first and Chambers Street. In the back of the furniture store there. That's where their headquarters are. Please, no more killing. Just let us go. Save your souls, young men. I am begging you." He whimpered with snot running out of his nose and into his mouth.

Kilroy came over and extended his gun. "How sure are you, old man? And don't lie to me. Your life depends on this shit."

"I am sworn to the truth. I will not lie under any circumstances. It's where they are. Ramone has taken over for their Posse after the death of Pablo. He swears that his crew will not rest until his crew seeks revenge for Pablo's death. He comes here once a week to repent and ask for his penance. Please, end this war. Save your souls, my children. It's not too late. I believe—"

Boom! Kilroy squeezed his trigger, leaving his gun smoking, knocking the priest backward before his head fell forward into his lap like Pablo's wife.

"Fucked up them bitches had more heart than he did. I never fucked with all that religious shit anyway. Fuck dude. Y'all kill everybody in here and let's get a move on." He said, stepping in front of the next female, pressing his barrel to her forehead and pulling the trigger, blowing her scalp off.

"Yo, I'll meet you niggas in the truck. I ain't killing no broad or no child. This shit foul, my nigga. We need to be going at they niggas. Ain't no good gon' come from this, trust me." I said, turning my back to them and making my way back up the church steps.

I had to get out of there or I was going to break up all that shit because, in my opinion, there should have been no reason that we killed them shorties or the females when we'd already been given the information of where the Mexican Posse's headquarters were, and who was calling for their crew now. My mind was focused in on bodying Ramone. Cutting the head off of the snake before I finished Nico in a sadistic fashion.

Gunfire began to ensue in the basement below, just as I opened the backdoor of the church and made my way toward our awaiting stolen GMC truck, saying a silent prayer in my head, asking for forgiveness for the things that was taking place down there.

Chapter 14

"I don't give a fuck about them bitches or them kids. Them fuck niggas could have hit my shorty or my baby's mother. They didn't care, so why should we?" Kilroy asked, loading bullets into the hundred-round clip of his M-4.

I sat across from him doing the same thing with blue latex gloves on my hands. I shook my head. "Long as I been in the game, lil' homey, I ain't ever went at no niggas's woman or his child. To me, that's bitch shit. It's the same thing that that fool Nico did, and it's one of the reasons we both wanna take his head off." I slammed the clip into my M-4 and cocked it. I looked the weapon over in my hand and curling my upper lip before looking around the room at the rest of our crew, who was doing the same thing to their assault rifles.

It was two in the morning, the night after our crew had massacred the Mexican Posse's women and kids. I figured that it would be smart for us to go at them the same night 'cause if they were real killas, they would have been together like we were plotting and trying to get their gameplans in order. I was hoping that they were all at their headquarters, maybe wondering why their women had not gotten at them as of late.

Before our crew had left the church, we made sure that we chained the downstairs doors where the murders had taken place. So, even if someone had managed to break into the church, they would not be able to get into the basement without a major hassle. On top of that, I was also watching my phone and

Facebook to see if the victims had been discovered. So far, we were in the clear.

Kilroy mugged me and sucked his teeth. "Yo, it sound like you trying to say I just gave the order for our crew to be on some bitch shit. Is that what you saying, my nigga?" He asked, setting his M-4 to the side of him and looking me over with anger.

I nodded. "That's exactly what I'm saying. Take that shit how you want to, but we gotta be smarter and use our fire power better than we just did. Next time, I'mma break that shit up. From here on out, we ain't killing no kids or no females unless we really have to. That's just that." I said, crushing up four Percocet 30's and placing the powder into four lines, sifting through it with an Ace of Spades playing card.

Kilroy sucked his teeth and shook his head. "Yo, you might be right. I may have given a bogus order, but seeing my daughter in tears like that, knowing who'd caused her that pain, made me not give a fuck about their bitches and kids. My lil' one only twenty-two months old and she's traumatized already. Fuck that, I would've eaten they shorties with a knife and a fucking fork if I had to. That's my lil' girl. Point-blank, period."

The backdoor opened. I looked over my shoulder to see Lenox come into the basement with his arm around a Mexican dude's neck, and a .40 caliber to the side of his temple.

"Yo, here this bitch nigga go right here. Even though he saying he'll cooperate, I ain't taking no chances. Any nigga that will sellout his crew ain't to be trusted. Get yo' bitch ass in there and tell the bosses what's good." Lenox said, throwing him in front of the couch where he fell to his knees.

All twenty of the Shooters that were present stood up and aimed their guns directly at him after cocking them loudly.

I stood up and kicked him in the chest, then held my M-4 to his nose while he laid on his back with his hands extended over his head in total submission. "Bitch ass nigga, is it true that your crew's headquarters is on thirty first and Chambers?"

"Yes, man. Holy fuck, yes. Please, don't kill me. I thought I came so I could strike a deal. Kilroy, you promised, Homes." He said, shaking like a leaf.

Just seeing him nut up like a bitch made me wanna knock his fucking head off, sit down and toot my pills. I needed to be numbed. I was starting to miss my mother and Whitney again and I didn't feel like breaking down.

Kilroy looked down at him and shook his head. "Calm yo' soft ass down, I know what I told you. Now, tell me where all of them are at this moment. And you bet not lie."

I walked over to him and put the barrel of his M-4 into his eye.

The Mexican swallowed and took a deep breath. "They upstairs from the furniture store, having a meeting. Earlier today, we went and got a bunch of mattresses because we were planning on shooting up as many of you guys as possible and the order is that nobody separates or goes home until the job is done. That order came up from the bosses back in Mexico City. They know about your gang, Kilroy. They also know about him and Pappa." He said, lowering his voice.

I frowned. "Me? How the fuck they know about me?" I asked, confused, and not even knowing who his bosses were.

"Pablo's father is head of the Muerte Cartel. He's the one that gave Pablo the money and narcotics to start his own cartel here in the states. As soon as Pablo was murdered, he demanded to know who was behind the killing, and that imformation was provided by your former right hand man, Nico. Your name is Jayden and I know for a fact that you won't be alive for long. You have a target on your back bigger than a police officer that's sent to a prison full of cop-killers."

Kilroy kicked him in the ribs so hard that he rolled over onto his stomach. "Muthafucka, ain't nobody ask yo punk ass all that." He kneeled and turned him back over, putting a knee to his chest. "What type of weapons do you bitches have?"

The Mexican coughed and winced in pain. "We got everything, even grenades. It won't be long until you niggers are blown off the map. But I don't want no parts of this shit. Leave me out of it." He said, trying to catch his breath.

Things weren't making sense to me. "Wait a minute, if y'all got all of this shit, then why the fuck are you here rolling over on your crew? That don't make sense to me. Do it to you, Kilroy?"

Kilroy laughed. "Aw, yeah, it makes sense. You see, we got both of this fool's twins, along with his mother and grandmother. If he makes any false moves, we'll kill them all with no remorse. Just like

I was telling you. The only way you get low-life bitch niggas to respond, kid, you gotta hit they ass below the belt where it hurts. This punk is a mama's boy. He'll do anything to keep her alive, along with his kids. His baby's mother died giving birth to them, so they are all that he has right now. Am I right Umberto?" Kilroy asked, half laughing.

Umberto nodded. "I don't want anything to do with this war, man. I came over to the States to give my family a better life. This is old world bullshit. I don't have time for it. Now, I've given you all that I know. Please, release me and my family. I promise to never speak a word of this to the cartel or the Posse." He looked from Kilroy then back over to me with pleading eyes.

"You sure they are there, right now? Keep in mind that your family's lives are on the line." He said, lowering his eyes.

Umberto nodded. "On my babies' lives, they are. They are having one last feast before they give you guys all that they have."

Me and Kilroy locked eyes and I knew what we had to do.

* * *

I pulled the gloves until they felt tighter on my fingers, then I adjusted my mask as I kneeled beside the the door that lead into the furniture store's back entrance. I looked over to the truck just as Kilroy got out of it with Umberto. He had him by the collar of his shirt, handling him aggressively, while the rest of the Shooters filed out of their vans and whips, lining themselves around the entrance to the furniture store.

It was four thirty in the morning, and so hot that I was sweating already. Where we were stationed, there were a bunch of gnats flying around, irritating the fuck out of me. We were set to enter from the back of the store where there was a case of metal stairs that lead upstairs. Once there, Umberto would use his key to get into the door. Having been plugged with Pablo and his crew ever since they were back in Mexico, I guessed that they trusted him more than they should have, even though I didn't for one second. I was looking for a reason to knock the top of his head off. I didn't like how much of a snitch he was. The fact that he could sellout his own crew didn't sit well with me. He reminded me of Nico— a bitch-snitch type of nigga. All them types, in my opinion, deserved to swallow lead.

Kilroy walked him to the stairs, then held his M-4 to his back and walked behind him as he made his way up the stairs slowly, taking one at a time while me and some of the Shooters stood and watched to make sure that we weren't blindsided, even though it was so early in the morning.

I made sure that I peeped all around through the scope on top of my M-4, and I couldn't see anything out of the ordinary. As soon as they were at the top of the stairs, me and five of the Shooters slowly made our way up that way, continuing to be on high alert. I still didn't understand what we were up against, but I'd heard the phrase cartel before when referring to the vicious mafias out of Mexico, so I knew that these dudes were not to be taken lightly. We had to vanquish they ass and knock them out of the picture like ASAP.

I made it all the way to the top of the stairs, just as Umberto was sliding the key into the lock, looking over his shoulder at Kilroy with a sad expression on his face. Once again, I wanted to blow his head off from being so soft. How was it that he was the one setting up his own crew, yet he was the one sad? I shook my head and kneeled beside the door, trying to figure out how the women of their crew had more heart than he did.

Umberto slowly turned the key, then pushed the door in with Kilroy right behind him. He still had his arm around Umberto's neck, guiding him inside as soon as the door was wide enough for the both to fit through. "Let's go, y'all." He forced him further inside and I waved for four of the Shooters to go in behind them.

Before I stood up, gunfire erupted. *Boom. Boom. Boom. Da-doom, da-doom, da-doom. Pop, pop, pop, pop, pop, pop.* I ducked all the way down and then jumped up to get ready to run inside, when Umberto came running out of the door with his eyes bugged out of his head. He seemed to bump right into me, knocking me backward. I slammed the barrel of my M-4 into his stomach and squeezed the trigger, letting three bullets chop into him. They exited out of his back. He fell over to the side before going over the railing, falling two stories to the ground.

More of the Shooters ran inside of the Mexican Posse's headquarter's as more and more gunfire ensued. I gathered myself, kneeled and took a deep breath. I was trying to let as much shooting go on as possible before I got involved. I wanted Kilroy and the Shooters to do most of the work, then I'd come in in the end and finish the job. Fuck that. In my opinion, that night wasn't the night to be getting shot. So, I waited there for a full two minutes after I'd killed Umberto, then I got down on my stomach and slithered into the door with my eyes wide. The first thing I noticed was that it was heavy with gunsmoke and the scent of burnt flesh and feces. I imagined that the Mexicans had gotten caught off guard, and because of that, it had caused most of them to shit on themselves while they were under attack which was understandable.

Kilroy stood over a bed full of them a short distance ahead of me, with his M-4 leveled downward and fire spitting from its barrel. *Boom, boom, boom, boom.* I watched the machine gun jumping in his hands before he ducked as bullets flew his way from one of the rival crew members who had flipped over a wooden table and took aim at the homey. I fired and put two big holes in the table, as one of the Shooters fell beside me with a hole in his face. He dropped his M-4 and I watched it slide across the floor.

More shots came in my direction. I couldn't tell from where though. *Boom, boom, boom, boom. Peeyun! Pee-yun!* Bullets slammed into the door that we'd come through. I slid on my belly until I was on the side of their refrigerator. Kilroy continued to trade bullets with the man behind the table as one of the Shooters put a few holes in another Mexican that ran out into the hallway with a Uzi in his hand. The Shooter's bullets stood him straight up. I literally watched the holes appear on his body before he fell face-first with a puddle of blood formed around him.

"Ahhhh! You muthafuckas!" The one from behind the table hollered, jumping up and running at Kilroy, bussing both of his hand pistols. His face was screwed into a mug with slobber dripping off of his bottom lip. It was visible, even through the fog of the gunsmoke. He looked as if he'd lost his mind.

Kilroy fell to his back and squeezed the triger on his M-4 again and again, but no bullets came out. His eyes got bucked, just as the Mexican made it within six feet of where he was, aiming his gun directly at Kilroy. Kilroy covered his head with his arms.

The other Shooters were still in an intense battle with other members of the rival crew. I don't think that they were able to see what was going on. It was like it all happened in slow motion. The Mexican ran and stopped, standing over Kilroy with his eyes lowered. He extended his arm.

Boo-wa! Boo-wa! Boo-wa! My bullet shot out of my M-4 and slammed into his temple, knocking the side of his face off before making him twist in the air and falling on his ass with blood shooting out of the hole in his head. I continued to look through the scope until I was sure that he was dead.

Only then did I run over to Kilroy, bussing my gun down the hallway, before ducking and sliding him my .45. "Here, nigga! Let's get the fuck up out of here!" I yelled.

He nodded and lowered his eyes, looking upward and bussing his gun. *Boom. Boom. Boom.* One of the Mexicans had caught two to the chest, flying backward. Kilroy aimed at another one, and bussed again, while more of the Shooters ran inside and got to emptying their weapons. They were chopping down the Mexicans one and two at a time. I popped as many as I could through my scope until I was out of bullets. Once that happened, I broke up out that bitch and ran to the truck. Bullshit wasn't about nothing.

* * *

An hour later, we were back at one of our traps in DC with me sitting on the couch, sipping from a bottle of Hennessy. I was shook. We'd lost five of the Shooters and killed up more than fifteen of the Mexican Posse niggas. I knew for a fact that it was about to be all over the news, and once word got back to their heads in Mexico, we were about to be in for it.

I had to get the fuck out of Philly. I needed to body that nigga Nico to close off that loose end, and then I was going to live a life with Myeesha after we hit that major lick she had lined up for me down there. I couldn't wait. I was missing her more and more lately, anyway. Plus, I wanted to put them Atlanta niggas on they heels, too. I even considered bringing Kilroy and some of the Shooers down there with me.

Kilroy paced with two pistols in his hand. He kept taking one deep breath after the next. "Yo, I can't believe you just saved my life, kid. That Mexican was finna blow my scalp off. He had me right where he wanted me, and I couldn't do shit. Yo, I owe you my soul, dunn. Word is muthafuckin' bond, kid." He shook his head and swung a pistol at the air. "Fuck! That was close!" He shook his head some more, then plopped down on the couch. He reached under it and pulled out a plate full of heroin, getting ready to toot his cares away.

Lenox stood up and grabbed his stomach. "Yo, I lost my lil' cousin back there, kid. Son was only fifteen. I don't know what I'mma tell my aunty. They just moved out here from Detroit to get away from all that killing and shit. Fuck, she gon' be hurt." He said, reaching for the bottle of Hennessy after I offered it to him.

"Son, that could've been you back there. Be thankful that it wasn't and that you get to live to murder another day. Nah'mean." I said before leaning my head down and tooting up a hard line of Percocets.

I needed to be numb more than ever because I felt the soul of Umberto scratching at me, along with the other Mexican I'd killed. That was one thing about me. Whenever I killed something, it was like the soul of the person that I'd bodied tended to get at me for a few weeks until I either killed somebody else, or just didn't feel that shit no more. But I always felt it. I didn't know why that was.

Kilroy tooted the line of heroin hard, then pulled on his nose, swallowing and sniffing loudly. "Yo, on my daughter, the city finna be on fire. If we gon' go at that fool Nico, then we gotta hurry up before that window close. You already know how the feds get down, kid. You know we gotta be on they watch list after all of this shit. Word to my mother." He leaned down and tooted up another thick line.

Lenox had four Oxy pills that he placed a playing card over, before crushing them up using the bottom of the Hennessy bottle. I could tell that he wanted to get high so he could be far away from the loss of his little cousin. I'd been there before. Infact, I was still there. It was one of the reasons I had my head lowered to the table, snorting as hard as I possibly could. I didn't even know if I was going to bury my mother or have her cremated. Her case had yet to flash across the television screen so I figured that she hadn't even been discovered as of yet. I'd told Myeesha to keep her mouth shut until she saw it posted on Facebook or one of the news outlets up here in Philly, and through tears, she agreed.

"Yo, you most definitely right, son. But don't even trip. I'mma take it to that nigga well before we meet up at Wilson's. I got this shit. Y'all just fall back and watch me work, then me and you got some business we need to talk about, Kilroy. I even got a slot for you too, Lenox, if y'all wanna fuck with me on some other shit." I leaned down and tooted up the last line of Percocets as hard as I could, trying my best to numb the pains in my heart but coming up shorter than a mosquito's penis.

I was higher than a muthafucka though as I pulled out my phone and hit Nico's cell, setting the date of two days from that night, so we could meet up at Wilson's gym and fight to the death, the Philly way, though I had a trick up my sleeve.

"Yo, word is bond, Jayden, you saved my life kid, so I'm indebted to you for as long as I'm alive. Whatever you feeling you need from me, on my daughter, son, you got it." He cocked his pistol and mugged me with obvious loyalty.

Lenox looked up and nodded with powder all over his face. I knew just how I was going to use both niggas, and I couldn't wait to get shit kicked off.

Ghost

Chapter 15

It didn't take Nico long to respond to my text, talking a bunch of bullshit, saying that he would be there, and I had better be too before he hung up and left me with a serious mug on my face. I loved the fact that the nigga was so cocky that he felt he was above the slums of Philly. Even though it irritated me to my soul, and always had ever since we were kids, I knew that I could use it to my advantage, which is what I planned on doing as I felt the rain beat down on my back.

I kneeled, took the bolt cutters and snapped the master lock that was on Janet's cellar, watching it fall to the ground while I picked the extra pieces up and threw them in the grass. Lightning flashed over my head. The wind picked up and started to blow so hard that I had to close my eyes because it made the rain crash into them, causing me to blink more than I wanted to.

After I picked the pieces of the lock out of the hinges that kept the cellar closed, I pulled open the latch and gradually got the doors opened, listening to them creak loudly in the night. I looked over my shoulder and nodded at Kilroy. He ran from the side of the garage and into the cellar with a .45 in his right hand. I waited until he disappeared down the stairs before I followed, closing the doors back as to not cause any attention to us entering into Janet's house this way.

When I got to the bottom of the flight of stairs, Kilroy was swatting at a big spider web that had been spun. It had so many wrapped bug inside of it that, as

I helped him, I could feel the different sizes of the spider's catch. It gave me an eerie feeling.

"Yo, I hate spiders, son. I feel like it's something crawling on me right now." Kilroy said, slapping the back of his neck and scratching his exposed arms.

Seeing him do all that shit had me itching. I tried to snap out of it and regain my focus, but I had the hee-bee gee-bees. There was a reason that we never came into Janet's basement. It was because of how many spiders were down there along with their big ass webs. The first time I had seen her basement, I'd left and went back upstairs, freaked out, vowing to never go down into the muhfucka again.

I finished scratching my arms and settled myself mentally before swatting and tearing down another web that looked to be bigger and fuller than the last one. After I ripped it down and picked some of it's contents off my gloves, I made my way to the stairs that led into Janet's house with Kilroy behind me, picking strands of the spider web off of his wet clothes. I think because of how wet we were that it made things feel that much itchier, but I didn't have time to pay attention to that.

I slowly crept up the stairs, trying my best to put as less pressure on them as I could. I was happy with the fact that they weren't squeaking as much. Halfway up, there was one noisy stair. I paused on it, gritting my teet, and holding up a hand to Kilroy, then pointing down as if to let him know to avoid that step. He outweighed me by at least forty pounds, so I could only imagine how much noise he would've made. We couldn't take that chance. Not this night.

I continued to travel up the stairs until I had the door's handle in my hand, turning it slowly before looking over my shoulder to see Kilroy avoid the noisy step, then rush up them until he was standing right behind me.

I slowly opened the door, then stuck my head into the house, looking around. The heavy scent of Syracuse Loud was in the air. I could hear Mary J. Blige singing out of the speakers that were upstairs, serenading the house with her version of "Sweet Thang". I smiled under my mask then lowered my eyes. As I was stepping into the hallway, looking to my right and then left, I could feel the rain's water slide down my back. I took the .9-millimeter off my waist and began to walk to my left toward the staircase that led upstairs. I pointed to the right for Kilroy to search that portion of the house. He nodded and crouched down, staying as low to the ground as possible, while I looked up the stairs with my heart pounding in my chest.

I didn't know why I kept on seeing images of my mother lying on her kitchen floor with her throat slit. My mind would jump from that image of her to the one of Whitney lying in the middle of the highway, twisted. I felt light-headed and had to snap out of it and focus on the task at hand. After I completed this, I would break out to Atlanta, fuck over the lick that Myeesha had waiting for me there, then set up shop in the south and get my money all the way up.

I was thinking of starting my own branch of the Shooters. A branch that would be about their paper to the utmost, but at the same time be down to destroy and conquer all our foes. I wanted to be filthy rich and powerful and wasn't nobody finna stand in the way of that. The lick with Myeesha would set me on the right path. I couldn't wait to hit Atlanta with a vengeance.

I tip-toed up the carpeted stairs slowly, holding on to the banister so I could put as less pressure on each stair as possible. The closer I got to the top, the louder the music got, and so was the smell of sex. It smelled like somebody had been fucking for at least an hour straight, and I didn't understand how that could be when the house was so fucking hot. It felt like it was every bit of eighty degrees inside of it, as the lightning flashed outside, and the thunder roared violently.

I cocked the hammer on my .9 as soon as I got to the top of of the stairs. Then, I crouched and made my way down the hallway where I could hear heavy breathing, moaning, and bed springs squeaking loudly. I smiled and lowered my eyes, jogging just a bit so I could make it down the hall to Janet' s room that was at the end of it. As soon as I got there, I noticed that the door was slightly ajar. I stood with my back against the wall, right outside of it, taking a deep breath before slightly nudging it open. In doing so, the sight inside totally blew my mind and caused my heart to skip a beat again.

I couldn't believe my luck as I forced my way into her bedroom after taking my other .9 off my hip and extending it toward the bed where Janet sat atop Nico, riding him while holding on to the top of the headboard with her face pointed toward the ceiling. She was riding him so hard that the headboard constantly knocked into the wall behind it.

I lowered my eyes and curled my lip. "Well, well, well. Look at what we have here."

To be continued...
Rotten to the Core 3
Coming Soon

Submission Guideline.

Submit the first three chapters of your completed manuscript to ldpsubmissions@gmail.com, subject line: Your book's title. The manuscript must be in a .doc file and sent as an attachment. Document should be in Times New Roman, double spaced and in size 12 font. Also, provide your synopsis and full contact information. If sending multiple submissions, they must each be in a separate email.

Have a story but no way to send it electronically? You can still submit to LDP/Ca$h Presents. Send in the first three chapters, written or typed, of your completed manuscript to:

LDP: Submissions Dept
Po Box 870494
Mesquite, Tx 75187

DO NOT send original manuscript. Must be a duplicate.

Provide your synopsis and a cover letter containing your full contact information.

Thanks for considering LDP and Ca$h Presents.

Coming Soon from Lock Down Publications/Ca$h Presents

BOW DOWN TO MY GANGSTA

By **Ca$h**

TORN BETWEEN TWO

By **Coffee**

BLOOD STAINS OF A SHOTTA **III**

By **Jamaica**

STEADY MOBBIN II

By **Marcellus Allen**

BLOOD OF A BOSS **V**

By **Askari**

LOYAL TO THE GAME **IV**

By **T.J. & Jelissa**

A DOPEBOY'S PRAYER **II**

By **Eddie "Wolf" Lee**

IF LOVING YOU IS WRONG… **III**

LOVE ME EVEN WHEN IT HURTS

By **Jelissa**

TRUE SAVAGE **V**

By **Chris Green**

BLAST FOR ME **III**

ROTTEN TO THE CORE **III**

By **Ghost**

ADDICTIED TO THE DRAMA **III**

By **Jamila Mathis**

LIPSTICK KILLAH **III**

CRIME OF PASSION **II**

By **Mimi**

WHAT BAD BITCHES DO **III**

By **Aryanna**

THE COST OF LOYALTY **II**

By **Kweli**

SHE FELL IN LOVE WITH A REAL ONE **II**

By **Tamara Butler**

LOVE SHOULDN'T HURT **III**

By **Meesha**

CORRUPTED BY A GANGSTA **III**

By **Destiny Skai**

A GANGSTER'S CODE III

By **J-Blunt**

KING OF NEW YORK II

By **T.J. Edwards**

CUM FOR ME **IV**

By **Ca$h & Company**

Available Now

RESTRAINING ORDER **I & II**

By **CA$H & Coffee**

LOVE KNOWS NO BOUNDARIES **I II & III**

By **Coffee**

RAISED AS A GOON I, II, III & IV

BRED BY THE SLUMS I, II, III

BLAST FOR ME I & II

ROTTEN TO THE CORE I II

By **Ghost**

LAY IT DOWN **I & II**

LAST OF A DYING BREED

BLOOD STAINS OF A SHOTTA I & II

By **Jamaica**

LOYAL TO THE GAME

LOYAL TO THE GAME II

LOYAL TO THE GAME III

By **TJ & Jelissa**

BLOODY COMMAS I & II

SKI MASK CARTEL I II & III

KING OF NEW YORK

By **T.J. Edwards**

IF LOVING HIM IS WRONG…I & II

By **Jelissa**

WHEN THE STREETS CLAP BACK I & II III

By **Jibril Williams**

A DISTINGUISHED THUG STOLE MY HEART I II & III

LOVE SHOULDN'T HURT I II

By **Meesha**

A GANGSTER'S CODE I & II

By J-Blunt

PUSH IT TO THE LIMIT

By **Bre' Hayes**

BLOOD OF A BOSS **I, II, III & IV**

Ghost

By **Askari**

THE STREETS BLEED MURDER **I, II & III**

THE HEART OF A GANGSTA I II& III

By **Jerry Jackson**

CUM FOR ME

CUM FOR ME 2

CUM FOR ME 3

An **LDP Erotica Collaboration**

BRIDE OF A HUSTLA **I II & II**

THE FETTI GIRLS **I, II& III**

CORRUPTED BY A GANGSTA I & II

By **Destiny Skai**

WHEN A GOOD GIRL GOES BAD

By **Adrienne**

A GANGSTER'S REVENGE **I II III & IV**

THE BOSS MAN'S DAUGHTERS

THE BOSS MAN'S DAUGHTERS II

THE BOSSMAN'S DAUGHTERS III

THE BOSSMAN'S DAUGHTERS IV

THE BOSS MAN'S DAUGHTERS **V**

A SAVAGE LOVE **I & II**

BAE BELONGS TO ME

A HUSTLER'S DECEIT I, II

WHAT BAD BITCHES DO I, II

By **Aryanna**

A KINGPIN'S AMBITON

A KINGPIN'S AMBITION **II**

I MURDER FOR THE DOUGH

By **Ambitious**

TRUE SAVAGE

TRUE SAVAGE II

TRUE SAVAGE **III**

TRUE SAVAGE **IV**

By **Chris Green**

A DOPEBOY'S PRAYER

By **Eddie "Wolf" Lee**

THE KING CARTEL **I, II & III**

By **Frank Gresham**

THESE NIGGAS AIN'T LOYAL **I, II & III**

By **Nikki Tee**

GANGSTA SHYT **I II &III**

By **CATO**

THE ULTIMATE BETRAYAL

By **Phoenix**

BOSS'N UP **I , II & III**

By **Royal Nicole**

I LOVE YOU TO DEATH

By Destiny J

I RIDE FOR MY HITTA

I STILL RIDE FOR MY HITTA

By **Misty Holt**

LOVE & CHASIN' PAPER

By **Qay Crockett**

TO DIE IN VAIN

Ghost

By **ASAD**

BROOKLYN HUSTLAZ

By **Boogsy Morina**

BROOKLYN ON LOCK I & II

By **Sonovia**

GANGSTA CITY

By **Teddy Duke**

A DRUG KING AND HIS DIAMOND I & II

A DOPEMAN'S RICHES

By Nicole Goosby

TRAPHOUSE KING I II & III

By **Hood Rich**

LIPSTICK KILLAH **I, II**

CRIME OF PASSION

By **Mimi**

STEADY MOBBN'

By **Marcellus Allen**

<u>BOOKS BY LDP'S CEO, CA$H</u>

<u>TRUST IN NO MAN</u>

<u>TRUST IN NO MAN 2</u>

<u>TRUST IN NO MAN 3</u>

<u>BONDED BY BLOOD</u>

<u>SHORTY GOT A THUG</u>

<u>THUGS CRY</u>

<u>THUGS CRY 2</u>

<u>THUGS CRY 3</u>

<u>TRUST NO BITCH</u>

<u>TRUST NO BITCH 2</u>

<u>TRUST NO BITCH 3</u>

<u>TIL MY CASKET DROPS</u>

<u>RESTRAINING ORDER</u>

<u>RESTRAINING ORDER 2</u>

<u>IN LOVE WITH A CONVICT</u>

<u>Coming Soon</u>

BONDED BY BLOOD 2

BOW DOWN TO MY GANGSTA

CPSIA information can be obtained
at www.ICGtesting.com
Printed in the USA
LVHW080639191120
672141LV00027B/310